Willow Tree

BY

Jo Ellen Miller

Published by Joemil Publishing Greenville, SC

ISBN: 978-0-578-28938-0 First printing April 2022
Printed in U.S.A.

The Purdue OWL Family of Sites. The Writing Lab and OWL at Purdue and Purdue U, 2008, owl.english.purdue.edu/owl. Accessed 23 Apr. 2008.

The Great Migration. History.Com Editors, 2021, www.history. com/topics/black-history/great-migration. Accessed 28 June. 2021

Dedication

I dedicate this novel to my late mother Susie Redmond whose strength and strong will has been and will always be a source of inspiration to me; to my late mother-in law, Myrtle Wright, whose feet I could sit at for hours and listen to her life stories; to my late aunts and uncles who took the migration path from the south to the north; (Aunts) Nell Stewart, Nettie Muse, Louise Flippin, Lutisha McCullough, Gladys McCullough, Ella Emerson, and my (living) aunt Agnes McDowell. My (Uncles) Robert Lee, Lee Henry, Ralph, and Jimmy McCullough.

And finally, I dedicate this novel to my late husband Alfred Miller who always supported me in all my endeavors and encouraged me with my writings. I continue to feel that his love and support surrounds me.

Epigraph

During the early part of the twentieth century more than 6 million African Americans relocated north during the great migration. For many it was a means for better economic opportunities as well as to escape the demeaning segregation laws.

"…Sometimes it can be tough when you got to choose between following your heart or following your dreams. Sometimes you end up paying a price whichever way you go…"

Acknowledgements

I would like to thank God for giving me the inspiration to write this novel and the nudge to complete it when I wanted to give it up.

I also want to thank my daughter, Venus, who's been the support I needed by reading my rough drafts and offering her thoughtful opinions and inputs and my son Cameron and granddaughter Keilah for offering their enthusiastic support and well wishes.

1

Maggie glanced out the open screenless window next to her and watched her two younger sisters, nine-year-old Lulu and seventeen-year-old Bernita help their mother sweep the front yard clean of leaves and debris. It wasn't a surprise to her to see Bernita holding the straw broom with one hand while making a halfhearted attempt to sweep the leaves into a pile. Afterall, lazy was her middle name.

She took a deep breath and inhaled the sweet fragrance of honeysuckle that wafted in through the room then resumed her task. Spring had finally arrived after an unusually cold, bitter winter. The warmth of the sun and the fresh air made her joyful and cheerful, but the weather wasn't the only reason for her happy mood. She had the house to herself for a few hours without being pestered by her siblings. Her brothers, ten-year-old Buster, and fourteen-year-old Jed were helping their father clean cow manure out of the barn.

The dress she was engrossed in sewing for the annual spring dance was almost completed. Most things were hard to come by lately for the family and she felt lucky to have a good piece of cloth. The color of the cloth and fabric were perfect, and she had her father to thank for it. He knew how much she loved to sew. Sometimes he would barter for scraps of cloth for her at the general store with vegetables from his garden. On good days he might bring home enough material for her to make a couple of dresses with enough left over to sew outfits for her mother and sisters too.

When she was a little girl, she would sit on the floor engrossed as she watched her mother cut patterns out of newspaper and pin them to potato sacks. The pumping of the foot pedal along with the rapid motion of the needle as it punched through the fabric, making a whirling, rumbling sound, fascinated her. Even more to see the end results of a suitable dress created out of material that once held dirty white potatoes. Being a fast learner, it wasn't long before she sat at the machine sewing dresses herself but with a softer, nicer material.

Maggie's mind wandered to her father. She was pondering the best way to bring up the subject of her going to Philadelphia again when Bernita bounced into the room, disrupting her musing.

Her sister walked to the opposite side of the room and fell backwards on a small bed. After a few moments she said, "Good lord! You got to make all that racket right now?"

"Yep. It's impossible to sew without making noise,"

Maggie replied, without looking at her. "You better get off Jed's bed. He made it up nice and neat."

Bernita rolled over onto her side to face her. In a whiny voice, she said, "It not fair you get to sit on your butt all day while we have to work."

"I did all my chores early this morning. I churned the butter plus put some beans on for dinner. Besides, I have to finish my dress for the dance."

Bernita sat upright on the bed and tilted her head from one side to the other.

Crinkling her nose, she said, "You wearing something made out of that ugly cloth?"

Maggie puffed her cheeks and blew out a long stream of air. She'd had it with her sister's mean, snotty comments. So childish and immature, she thought to herself. No wonder people were always surprised when they found out that Bernita was just a year younger than her. Even Lulu acted more mature. She didn't like confrontations and usually did her best to avoid them, but it wasn't always an easy thing to do with Bernita. Her sister had a way of getting under her skin. But today she was determined not to let her spiteful attitude dampen her mood. Holding back her irritation, she said in a calm voice, "This the best material I ever got my hands on. Why don't you go find something to do, Bernita?"

"I'm resting. I'm tired from all the work Ma made me do."

"Well, you a bothering me. Oh, shoot!" Maggie angrily ripped a wayward thread from a seam. "See. You made me mess up!" She scowled at Bernita. "Stop pestering me!"

Mrs. Smith shuffled into the room, carrying a basket full of green leaves. Although a small frame woman, she plopped down in the worn-out armchair next to Maggie as if she was several pounds heavier. She set the basket down on the floor.

"The poke springing up fast this year. They all over the place." She wiped her hands on her dress and turned to Maggie. "How yo dress coming?"

"Almost finished, Ma." Maggie replied. She glanced over at Bernita sprawled on the bed and narrowed her eyes, "At least I will be If she stops interrupting me."

Ignoring Bernita's hateful glare, she pulled the dress from under the needle, snipped the thread and held it up eagerly. "What you think?"

"It's so pretty. It'll look nice on you," Mrs. Smith said. She then directed her attention to Bernita, who was lying on her side with her head propped up on a hand, watching them. "Why don't you let her sew you up a dress for the dance? She got enough cloth left over."

Bernita crinkled her nose and said in a haughty tone, "No. that material is ugly. Plus, she didn't even sew it right."

Maggie's eyebrows shot up in disbelief. "Well, wear one of your old tacky dresses for all I care!"

"It looks good to me," Mrs. Smith said. "Hold it up to you, Maggie."

Maggie stood and placed the lacy, high collar of the dress under her chin letting the rest of the dress fall just below her knees. The yellow and purple, floral print contrasted nicely with her jet-black hair, and her smooth, coffee brown skin.

Mrs. Smith's face was expressionless as she reached for the dress and inspected it from front to back. The sudden smile showed her approval. "These seams are good. Oh, you gonna stand out at that dance in this dress for sure."

Pleased from her mother's praise, Maggie grinned and twirled around the room while still holding the dress under her chin. Whether curtains for the windows or outfits for Lulu's dolls, it didn't matter. She enjoyed the thrill of creating and being appreciated for her skills.

"I remember the days when I used to cut a rug at the dances. Caught all the young fellows' attention," Mrs. Smith said with a laugh.

Maggie laughed along with her. She pictured her mother as a beautiful young girl with a swarm of men surrounding her waiting for a turn to dance. "Come on, Ma. Show us how you used to cut a rug in your day."

"Lordy. My bones too stiff now for all that silliness." She raised up from the chair with a grunt. "You go on and finish your sewing." Then to Bernita she said, "Help me wash up these greens for supper."

Bernita tumbled off the bed and gave Maggie a sidelong, hateful glance before following behind her mother.

***

The Smith family, noisy as usual, gathered around a long table in the corner of the kitchen for a sparse meal of cornbread, poke salad and pinto beans. The table, made from oak wood by Maggie's grandfather, had two long benches on either side. Mr. and Mrs. Smith sat on one side of the table with Buster and Lulu in between them. Maggie sat on the end of the opposite bench with Bernita and Jed.

There wasn't meat with their meals on weekdays. Meat was a luxury saved for Sundays unless the preacher stopped by for a visit or relatives showed up unannounced. On those special occasions a chicken would be chased down in the yard and prepared.

The rugged, quaint kitchen lacked in amenities such as running water, but the yellow painted walls gave it a bright and cheerful feeling. It was where Maggie spent a lot of happy days working alongside her mother: canning peaches, beans, corn, okra, and making plum jellies and preserves. To Maggie, the kitchen was similar to most folks she knew in the area.

A milk churn sat in one corner of the room. Herbs her mother found in the woods hung from a rafter suspended above the window to dry out. An assortment of wooden barrels that stored meal, flour, a variety of dried beans, and potatoes, lined a wall near the back door.

It was warm in the kitchen from the potbellied stove, but with the screenless back door open, a gentle breeze blew in from time to time. Three mutts, huddled under the house, peered up through the wood slates in the kitchen, eagerly waiting for Buster to drop them scraps of food.

Maggie listened as Jed and Bernita traded a barrage of insults as they piled their plates with food. Buster and Lulu, attempting to side with Jed, were no Match for Bernita's fast tongue. She only hushed long enough for her father to say grace. As soon as he said 'Amen,' she picked up again with her chattering.

Maggie usually joined in with her sibling's squabbles to offer her two-cents worth but tonight she had other things on her mind. She stirred through her food with her fork, barely eating.

"That there some good grub you messing over, Maggie," her father said, jarring her back to the present. "Something weighing on yo mind tonight?"

Maggie looked up and hesitated before speaking. What was on her mind tonight was the same thing that's been on her mind for a while now. She just wasn't sure if she should bring it up again. To her disappointment, whenever she'd asked before she always got a flat no for an answer.

Clearing her throat, she looked from one parent to the other. "Pa, have you and Ma given any more thought about me going to Philadelphia?"

The entire room suddenly became quiet, as her brothers and sister's full attention diverted to her.

Mr. Smith fork stopped in mid-air. "Maggie, we don been through this already."

She knew by the tone of his voice he was annoyed with her question, but she was persistent anyway. "I know, Pa. But it's the only way for me to better myself. You always talking about us kids having a better life than you and Ma had. It's my only chance," she pleaded.

"We just ain't ready yet, honey, for you to go traipsing off to some big city," her mother chimed in. "City life a whole lot different than what you used to. Maybe when you're a little bit older."

Maggie's words came out in a rush, "Rick did it. And he doing good for himself too. And…and Daisy can get me on at the sewing factory where she works. She said I could make good money. At least twenty dollars a week." She paused to search her father's face for any sign that her reasoning was getting through to him. Seeing none, she continued. "I know how hard things been on the farm. I can help out by sending money home. Please Pa. please Ma. Think about it some more."

"Me and yo Ma will talk about It," he said without conviction as if the conversation was over.

Feeling defeated, Maggie let out a small sigh. She just couldn't understand why he was so reluctant to let her go. They refused to consider her point of view and her plea wasn't getting her anywhere. She might as well had been talking to a rock. Maybe it was best to just put it aside for now, she thought.

"If Maggie go can I go too, Pa?" Bernita blurted out.

"We can't have both y'all taking off leaving at the same time. We need one of you to stay around here for a while at least."

Jed, not missing an opportunity to taunt Bernita, said, "Who gonna milk the cow in Maggie place if you ups and leaves?"

"It not my problem and I don't care!" Bernita replied flippantly.

"You have to. Milking is girls work," Buster said, stuffing a handful of cornbread in his mouth with one hand while dropping beans between the wood slates of the floor with the other one.

"And I'm not old enough yet," Lulu added.

Bernita banged her fists on the table. "I ain't milking no old cow!"

The commotion started all over again with Jed yelling, "Yes you is! I ain't doing it!"

Buster and Lulu chanted in unison, "Bernita got to milk the cow! Bernita got to milk the cow!"

To Maggie's relief, it didn't take long for her father to put a stop to it.

"Y'all hush! Cut it out. Now! Y'all a do what y'all told to do to help out around here, you hear?" And the reply back was a meek "Yass sum."

Her father, a tall, large man, knew how to keep order in his household just with his deep, booming, voice alone. Seldom did he have to use the switch on them. When he spoke they listen. He looked at Bernita and said in a calmer tone, "Now, we ain't decided if Maggie can go or not. But if she do, you gonna have to take on some of her chores along with getting yours done."

"She don't half do her chores as it is," Jed said, enjoying himself.

Bernita glared at him. "Ain't so. I do all my chores."

Mr. Smith drew his thick eyebrows together. "Jed, a hard head makes a soft behind," he said in a voice full of warning.

Jed lowered his head sheepishly, then scooped a forkful of food into his mouth.

"Maggie gets to do everything," she continued. "I want to get off this old farm too!"

"That's enough now," Maggie's mother said sternly.

She should learn to keep her mouth shut, Maggie thought to herself. She stayed in trouble enough with her constant griping and hissy-fits. Bernita was always trying to copy her. No matter what she wanted, Bernita had to have it too. Going up north hadn't even occurred to her until she asked to go. Of course, she really didn't care if her sister went to Philadelphia, but she agreed with her father. One of them needed to stay on the farm.

As everyone settled back to their meals, Maggie went back to her mental task of daydreaming. She'd had a longing to leave Hoop County ever since her older brother, Rick, left home to go north four years ago. When he came back for visits, he had such exciting things to tell them about the city that he made it seem like the Promised Land. It intrigued her. She wanted to see it all for herself. She wanted to bump elbows with the crowd of people on the street, shop in nice department stores, and ride the streetcars. But more than anything, she wanted to escape the drudgery of eking out a dull life on a farm in the south that wasn't always pleasant for colored folks.

It was a puzzle to her why her parents wouldn't want her to go. They both worked so hard to make ends meet on the farm, yet things seemingly kept getting worse than better. She noticed lately that the barrels were nearly empty most of the time. The extra money she could send back home would be a godsend for the family.

They had been sharecroppers up until five years ago when her father lucked up on ten acres of farmland that was selling dirt cheap. A house, big enough for the family, and a barn for raising livestock came with the property. He purchased it with the hard-earned money he had squirreled away from selling the vegetable he grew himself in a small plot and fresh eggs from the many laying hens that roamed the yard and finally got the family out of the system.

In their prior run-down log cabin, her and her siblings were constantly sick with hacking coughs and running noses due to the cold drafts that seeped through the walls in the winter. They would patch the cracks with paper torn out of the Sears catalogue books but with little success. The chilly, damp air always found a way in.

When the family moved into their crudely built, weather washed, white house with an upstairs and a loft, it was as if they had moved into a mansion. It didn't matter that they didn't have indoor plumbing. At least there were no more drafty winters, and the outhouse wasn't too far down the trail. Her father promised to one day add an indoor toilet and a water pump in the kitchen.

Maggie's father was proud to have his own land to farm. In the beginning, he brought in good profits with the vegetables he grew and sold at the market, but farming was backbreaking, hard work and no matter how hard you worked there were no guarantees of success. That's why she hated farming. A person's livelihood depended on a good harvest, and setbacks happened much too often.

Last year an unforeseen late frost destroyed the beans, and the following summer most of the corn perished when Hoop River overflowed. Because of the ongoing depression, that started three years ago, the crops that did survive, didn't bring in much cash. People just didn't have the money to spend. The winter months had been long and difficult for the family. Maggie and Bernita took turns helping their mother with the ironing she took in, but that barely brought in enough income. The most they earned was two dollars a week. Rick did his best with sending money home, but he had his own family to feed.

Her family fared better than most folks during those dark days, however. She heard stories of families being evicted from their homes when the landowners lost their farms to the bank. The depression ripped families apart. Men, women, and children roamed the countryside with sad, hungry eyes, begging for food. Maggie had seen a few people herself holed up in makeshift tents by the riverbank.

For the most part, though, people in Hoop County tried to look out for each other. Her mother alone donated plenty of her canned vegetables, jars of preserves, and jellies to hungry families. When a young couple who attended their church ended up evicted from their rental home, her parents took them in for a few days until they found a place to live. They had a six-month-old baby and two- and four-year-old toddlers. The Smith's household became cramped with the extra people, but Maggie was glad her family were able to help them.

She loved children and didn't mind helping care for the little ones. In fact, she carried the baby around so much that her mother warned her she would be spoiled. That didn't stop her from picking up the cute bundle of joy every time she whimpered. To her dismay, though, taking care of the baby put ideas in her mother's head. She told her that maybe it was high time she had some babies of her own.

She knew her mother wanted her to get married and start a family like most of the young women did when they reached a certain age in Hoop County. Lord knows she threw enough hints. Not that she didn't have suitors. Many single men were interested in her, but none of them piqued her interest.

Back in the fall, her mother tried to set her up with a young preacher from another county that she met at the church revival. "He got a house sitting on ten acres that his Pa left him," her mother said to her as if the best opportunity in her life had come along. "He a good catch. You ought to let him court you. Bout time for you to think about finding someone to settle down with."

Against her wishes, her mother started inviting him to Sunday dinners. And Preacher Todd didn't waste no time letting his intentions be known either. He proposed to her on his third visit.

Maggie couldn't see herself settling down with him or anyone else, at least not yet. Although she wanted a husband and children one day, she wasn't ready to be a wife and mother. Deep down inside, she felt something else was on the horizon for her. She just didn't know what. The young preacher didn't let up. He had set his eyes on her being his wife.

Maggie, although not wanting to be outright rude, resorted to doing subtle things to dissuade him. She would sit grim and only reply to him with short abrupt answers. But he was slow getting the message. When he tried holding her hand, she moved hers out of his reach and if he tried sitting close to her on the couch, she inched away from him. Eventually, after a month of his Sunday visits it sunk in that she wasn't interested, and he abandoned his courtship attempts.

Her mother had been disappointed, but Maggie had different plans and ambitions for herself. Her parents just didn't understand that, for her, life would be different.

"The spring dance is coming up this Saturday," Maggie's mother announced out of the blue, relieving the tension hovering over the table and snapping Maggie back to the present.

"Y'all young'uns planning on going?" Mr. Smith asked, directing his question to Jed, Bernita, and Maggie.

"I am," Maggie said as she got up from the table to scrape her uneaten food into the pan set aside for the pig.

"Not me," Jed said. "I'm gonna be setting rabbit traps in the woods."

Mr. Smith looked at Bernita. "What bouts you?"

Bernita, still fuming, nodded her head, yes.

"I expect both of you to stick together and come home together. Y'all hear?"

"Yass sum," they answered in unison. Maggie wished that just once she didn't have to be responsible for Bernita whenever they went somewhere. She could be such a pain with her childish behavior. She embarrassed her wherever they went. But rules were rules as far as her folks were concerned and she had to obey them.

"Maggie don made herself a nice dress from that material you brought home, Silas."

Her father smiled. "Our Maggie can sew her hiney off. I'm glad we fixed up that old Singer for her. I'm surprised she ain't worn it out yet."

2

The spring dance took place every year in a large, renovated barn that had been remodeled with clapboard, white paint, and a wood floor. A platform stood in the middle of the floor where musicians dished out popular tunes with their fiddles, guitars, a piano, and drums. People in the county and adjacent counties always looked forward to the grand event held the second weekend in April. The start of spring marked a new year of successful crops, and the dance was the perfect way to bring in the season with fellowship and good times.

The young and single had additional reasons for looking forward to the yearly dance. Except for the church picnic held annually in the fall, it was the only other social gathering where they had the opportunity to mingle with the opposite sex. They wouldn't dare pass up the opportunity to get spruced up in their best outfits in hopes of finding a potential mate.

Folks came in wagons, on horses, and by foot. Gaiety filled the air as throngs of people filed into the building, packing it full. Maggie was familiar with most of the people filtering in, several were from her church. There were a few new faces, however, that she didn't recognize which intrigued her. She enjoyed meeting new people.

Elderly women from the local churches stood guard behind long tables set up with savory macaroni and cheese, potato salad, ham, fried chicken, and cakes, along with other mouthwatering treats. Liquor wasn't allowed inside, so every so often a group of men would sneak out to the back of the building. Some of them would sneak back in a few minutes later walking with a slight stagger and with big silly grins on their faces. Maggie, as well as everyone else, knew a bottle of moonshine passed from hand to hand behind the building as if it was an unspoken ritual.

Old Man Neb, a wiry, seventy-five-year-old widower, was among the men who kept sneaking outside for 'a little juice', as he called it. He came back in after his last trip full of pep. He staggered to the middle of the empty dance floor and began entertaining the crowd with a lively buck dance as the fiddler played a tune. Everyone roared with laughter and cheered him on. Others joined him as the fervor caught on, kicking up their legs and flaying their arms to an innate rhythm they all shared.

Maggie stood off to the side with Bernita and two of their friends, Sarah, and Rosa, enjoying the scene. Guys walked up to the girls intermittently and extended their hands out as an offer to dance. Maggie turned down two young men who then turned their attention to the other girls in the group, who accepted the extended hands with no qualms.

"Maggie, why didn't you dance with Monroe?" Sarah asked after a young man led Bernita to the dance floor to join the throng of flapping, swirling bodies.

"He been after me to be his girl for the longest. If I give him one dance, he will hound me for the rest of the night. Same for Bruce. I don't want them to get ideas in their heads. I just want to enjoy myself tonight and not be pestered."

Sarah laughed. "Then maybe you shouldn't have taken such pains to look so pretty. A lot of eyes on you tonight."

A glimpse around the room verified Sarah's remarks: men stole glances her way; some furtive and some unabashed, including even those who had a female by their side. Her mother had been right. She attracted attention with her new dress and her hair pinned up in a bun with cascading ringlets framing her face. She fidgeted with her hair and smiled politely, but the men who she thought were halfway interesting didn't approach her. Men, Maggie mused, the ones you don't want to be bothered with are the ones brave enough to step forward.

Maggie spotted Bernita stomping around on the dance floor and thought to herself that if only Bernita would take the time to fix herself up, she could be much prettier. Her thick, dark brown wavy hair hung loosely down to her shoulders, and she had beautiful big, brown eyes that missed nothing. However, the gray and brown loose-fitting dress she chose for the night, looked as if it had had its share of wear.

She had offered Bernita one of her dresses, but Bernita being Bernita turned her nose up at the idea. Maggie let out a sigh. She will never get a boy to court her if she never learns how to be more presentable.

So far, the evening was enjoyable. Maggie just hoped Bernita would behave herself and not start any trouble with anyone. Last year she got into a heated argument with a girl from Marsh County. They were about to throw punches until she pulled her outside to cool off and threatened to tell her parents. That girl wasn't at the dance tonight but that didn't mean Bernita wouldn't start up with someone else.

Bernita came off the dance floor and joined Maggie, Rosa, and Sarah. "Whew! I'm sweating like a pig."

Maggie watched her peer around the room and knew it would be just a matter of time before she found some juicy gossip to share. She was constantly surveying the crowd then reporting back to them whatever dirt she could dig up.

As if on cue, Bernita pointed a finger towards the opposite corner of the room and said, "Look at Ollie over there. She thinks she's hot stuff."

Maggie pushed her finger down. "It's not polite to point at people."

Bernita pursed her lips in a pout. "Well, if I don't point, how will you know which way to look?"

"Where she at?" Sarah asked.

Bernita pointed with her head and said, "Over there."

Maggie turned her head along with the other girls. Across the room a young girl was engaged in a seemingly lively conversation with three young men.

"Huzzy," Rosa said with scorn.

"Yeah," Bernita echoed in agreement. "I ought to trip her if she walks by here again."

Bernita and her two friends laughed, but Maggie was appalled that her sister had it in her mind to do such a thing. "You need to stop being so childish, Bernita."

Unfazed, Bernita said "So. You aint my Ma. Stop acting like it."

Maggie opened her mouth to say something snide when she caught the eye of a handsome young man standing by the punch bowl a few feet away. Riveted by his gaze, she couldn't take her eyes off him.

Bernita, turning to see what suddenly caught Maggie's attention, became excited. She started tugging on Rosa's arm and in a loud whisper said, "That's him! That's him! Rosa! I can't believe it?"

With her eyes still on the handsome stranger, Maggie said, "Bernita, what in the world are you carrying on so about?"

"Clarence," she crooned.

Rosa's jaw dropped open. "The Clarence we met at the church picnic?"

"It's him alright. Oh, he's coming this way. Stop staring and being so obvious."

Sarah and Rosa immediately straightened their posture and patted their hair in place.

Maggie watched with anticipation as Clarence maneuvered his way through the crowd toward them.

When he got closer Bernita stepped out in front of her. "Hi, Clarence, remember me?" she gushed. When a puzzled look crossed his face, she said "Mount Zion picnic last fall?

Rock skipping contest?" she added.

"Oh, yeah. Yeah," Clarence said dismissively "Nice seeing you again." Then, looking around her he extended a hand to Maggie. "Care to dance?"

"Yes. I would love to." She didn't give the look of dejection on Bernita's face a second thought as she reached for his hand. In fact, she didn't even notice how hurt her sister looked because at that moment, no one else existed in the world but her and him.

She allowed Clarence to lead her to the dance floor where she fell into his arms with ease. He was even more handsome up close with a deep pool of dark, brown eyes and black, coarse, wavy hair cut close to his head.

"You a pretty good dancer," Clarence said as they swirled around on the dance floor to a blues ballad. "You always come to these shin digs?"

"I started coming three years ago with my parents. Last year was the first time they let me, and my sister come without them."

"They didn't come tonight?"

"No. They wasn't up to it." She paused, then said, "I don't recall ever seeing you here."

"First time for me. I ain't much for dancing. My cousin and his wife talked me into it."

"Well, for someone who ain't much for dancing, you doing mighty nice."

"Not bad for a person with two left feet, huh?" he replied with a laugh.

Maggie smiled. "No. Not bad at all."

"My name's Clarence, by the way."

"So, I heard. Mine's Maggie. Maggie Smith." People considered her tall at five feet, nine, but he had her by at least five inches. She didn't meet many men who were taller than her. Men didn't seem to grow tall in Hoop County.

"Well, Maggie Smith, I started to go fishing this evening. I'm glad I had a change of plans and came here instead."

"I'm glad you did too. You do much fishing?"

"Yep. Whenever I get a chance. You?"

"Fish? No. I hate fishing. I tried it a few times. Wasn't much fun."

"Maybe you just need the right person to show you how to cast a line," he said in a low, sexy voice.

Maggie sensed a hint of flirtation in his deep, smooth voice and she was enjoying it. Lowering her eyes, she replied, "Perhaps I do," She was aware of the slight pressure of his hand in the small of her back. A tingly sensation rippled from the base of her spine up to her neck causing her to feel flushed.

They continued the dance engaged in conversation and each other. After the song ended, Maggie began leading the way towards the group of girls.

"Where you live if you don't mind my asking?" Clarence inquired.

"Near the Jefferson's place. Not far from here."

"I know the area. Good farmland around there."

"Plenty of it."

"Think I can come visit you sometime?"

"I would like that," Maggie said, hoping he really meant it.

Clarence turned to go in the opposite direction. "See you around, Maggie Smith," he called out before disappearing into the crowd.

"Maggie, you lucky dog," Sarah said teasingly after he was no longer in sight.

"I get to dance with him next," Bernita said, as if it was an undisputed fact.

"Bernita, you can't dance with him unless he asks you." Bernita's lack of etiquette when it came to the opposite sex concerned her. She was such a tomboy who rarely gave boys a second thought except to fight with them. In Maggie's mind Bernita only wanted to dance with Clarence to compete with her as usual.

Bernita stuck her chin out and said, "Well, maybe he will ask me."

"He might," Maggie said halfheartedly but deep down she knew he would come back for her. She watched as Bernita panned the room with her eyes. She knew she was trying to spot him. It didn't perturb her, though. There were plenty of boys at the dance Bernita could choose from, but as far as Clarence was concerned, she had chosen him for herself.

When another song started up, Maggie felt someone tap her on her shoulder. She swung around to see him standing behind her with a broad grin on his face.

"Care for another dance? "

"Yes," she said sweetly then smiled triumphantly at Bernita as she joined his hand.

Maggie stayed by Clarence' side the rest of the night, forgetting all about her father's rule for her and Bernita to stay together. When they weren't on the dance floor, they were huddled in a corner of the room, talking, and getting to know each other better.

Girls would prance by giving Maggie hostile glares, their displeasure of her monopolizing an available male made obvious. Young men, whom she had rejected, paraded by her and Clarence to give her looks of disapproval, unhappy that she had chosen a stranger over one of them. Maggie wasn't fazed; she was with the person she wanted to be with and having the time of her life.

When the dance ended at eleven o'clock, people headed out in different directions. Bernita and Maggie had joined up with a group going their way. Maggie lingered behind with Clarence, aware that Bernita would get home before her. Hopefully she could get in the house before her father noticed they weren't together, but she enjoyed Clarence's company too much to be overly concerned. He accompanied her two of the three miles to her home. He promised to visit her soon, then took off to join his cousin and his wife going in the opposite direction.

3

"Benita," her father yelled out to her. "stop piddlin' and make yourself useful! You slow as molasses!"

A full moon, according to folk tale was the best time for planting if you wanted healthy, plentiful crops and Mr. Smith had a lot of plowing to do. He overturned the earth with a large plow hitched to two mules while Buster followed behind him dropping aged cow manure with gloved hands in the fresh grooves. Maggie, Mrs. Smith, and Lulu followed directly behind Buster sprinkling seeds in the enriched, furrowed soil. Jed's job was to come behind with a hoe to cover the seeds with dirt.

***

Bernita, whose job was to help Buster with the fertilizing, was instead in a world all her own. Saturday night was still fresh in her mind. Maggie had kept Clarence, her Clarence, all to herself and she was furious. She couldn't get it out of her mind and the more it stayed on her mind, the angrier she became. She had tried several times to get Clarence's attention, but to her dismay, he was so smitten by Maggie, he treated her as if she didn't even exist. Bernita kicked at a mound of dirt with her feet, then watched as it scattered into the air and spattered back to the ground. So unfair. She should have been the one he wanted to be with. After all, she claimed him first. Her thoughts led her back to that day when she saw him at the fall picnic. Maggie wasn't even there. She had stayed home with a bellyache.

She remembered that day well. Six wagonloads of people from different churches came to the picnic at Hoop River. It had been a beautiful autumn day. The vibrant red, yellow, orange, and golden leaves from the surrounding trees reflecting in the water created a serene, picturesque sight. She loved nothing more than being outdoors surrounded by nature, and she had been in her element.

When the last wagonload of people pulled up, she was wading in a shallow part of the river with her dress pulled up to her knees. He caught her attention right away sitting tall and handsome on the rim of the wagon with a big, floppy hat on his head and a long straw dangling from the corner of his mouth.

Mesmerized, she watched as he leapt over the side of the wagon and was still standing in the water with her dress pulled up above her knees when he walked by and tipped the brim of his hat in greeting.

"Howdy," he said.

Bernita smiled and nodded her head in greeting. Then realizing that she was exposing herself, she suddenly let go of her dress. It fell into the water soaking the hemline, but she didn't care. Her eyes traveled with him as he joined up with some other young men around his age.

Later that day Rosa said to her, "Go ahead. I dare you." When Bernita hesitated, Rosa urged her on. "Don't be a scary-cat. You like him, don't you?"

"Yeah."

"Then go on," Rosa urged, giving her a nudge.

Clarence was just a few feet away on the riverbank skipping stones across the water with a group of his friends.

Leaving Rosa spying behind a large oak tree, she sashayed up to him. Although not usually a shy person Bernita struggled to muster up enough courage to speak. "Hey," she said as she sat down beside him on the soft grass.

Clarence looked at her and grinned. "Hey back to you."

The sound of his voice was like butter. Soft and smooth. It was at that moment that she knew in her heart he was the one for her. She was at a loss as to what to say next and simply said, "Mind if I join you?" Clarence's friends snickered and taunted him, but she ignored them.

"Nope," Clarence said as he searched the ground for a stone.

"My name's Bernita by the way."

"I'm Clarence."

A moment of awkward silence elapsed between them. Bernita tried hard to come up with something clever to say but nothing came to mind. The only thing she could think to do was to grab a stone, throw it out as far as she could, and watch as it skimmed the surface creating rippling waves.

"Wow," Clarence exclaimed. "That went a long way. You pretty good."

His compliment relaxed her. It pleased her as well that her rock went out further than any of the boys. "You think it gonna rain?" she asked as she took aim with another stone.

Clarence looked up into the vast blueness of the sky. "Well, being that there ain't a cloud in the sky, I wouldn't say so."

Of course, it wasn't going to rain. She knew that. How foolish of her. Bernita looked over her shoulder toward the tree where Rosa was still hiding and said, "I gotta go. My friend is looking for me." She jumped up and ran to where Rosa had been observing everything from her hiding spot. They both collapsed behind the tree with uncontrollable giggling.

Bernita and Rosa inconspicuously followed Clarence the rest of that afternoon. They would quickly dash behind trees or a wagon when Clarence came close to spotting them.

When it was time for the crowd to eat their bagged lunches, Bernita and Rosa spread a blanket on the ground near Clarence and his friends. Not wanting to risk looking foolish again, she had been too skittish to approach him. She wasn't sure anyway if he was interested in her or not, but she could swear she saw him looking her way occasionally, which gave her a glimmer of hope. When the day's festivities were over, and everyone started packing up to leave, she walked up to him just before he hopped up on his wagon. "It was nice meeting you, Clarence," she said coyly.

He tipped his hat down and responded, "Nice meeting you too," then proceeded to join his group.

Bernita berated herself for not saying more to him, but they would meet again one day. She was sure of it.

After that day Bernita only saw Clarence again in her dreams. She often fantasized about him wrapping his strong arms around her shoulders and getting lost in the kisses of his full, soft lips. They were bound to meet again one day; she kept reassuring herself, and he would declare his undying love for her. She knew it was just a fantasy, but she held onto it nevertheless.

It looked like her long-held dream had finally come true when she saw him coming toward her at the dance. But when Clarence by-passed her for stuck-up Maggie her heart dropped. Feeling dejected, she shrunk back into the shadows. It was as if she didn't exist at all. The rest of the night was ruined for her.

Once again Maggie gets what she wants, Bernita thought bitterly. She reared her foot back and kicked a mound of dirt with such force it went flying high into the air, some of it falling to land in her hair. She flung her head wildly from side to side.

"Bernita!" her father called out again.

"I ain't got nothing to do, Pa!" Bernita yelled back. "Buster won't let me help him!"

"Here," Maggie offered as she straightened up and stretched backwards with a hand on her side. She held out a small, brown burlap bag. "You can help with these seeds."

"No. I don't want to," Bernita said with contempt as she pushed Maggie' hand away.

"You help Maggie, or you can plow the mules," Mrs. Smith said in a no-nonsense tone of voice.

Bernita snatched the bag out of Maggie' s hand and began throwing the seeds on the ground not caring how they landed.

She knew first-hand the wrath of her strict parents if any of them stepped too far out of line. She was the one who always got into the most trouble. Never Maggie though. The favorite child never did nothing wrong and never got as much as a talking to. A wry grin spread across Bernita's face as she thought about the time when she got a whipping for putting earth worms in Maggie' bed. Everything frightened prissy pants. But not her. She wasn't afraid of nothing.

Jed dug up the worms and insisted she be the one to put them in her bed and then he tattled on her when Maggie went crying to Ma and Pa. He escaped punishment by saying he had nothing to do with the prank. Such a liar. A sinister smile crept at the corners of Bernita's mouth. She recalled how she got even with Jed by punching him in the nose when she cornered him alone behind the house. Getting another whipping for bloodying his nose didn't faze her. Getting even had been worth it.

After another stern warning from her mother, Bernita calmed down and began dropping the seeds in a more uniform manner. Because of her antics, her parents were much stricter on her than the others. Bernita knew she needed to behave better, but no matter how hard she tried, she felt she would never be good enough. She wasn't Maggie. She gave up trying to be like her a long time ago.

4

Maggie was in the kitchen washing dishes with Lulu and Bernita when she heard a knocking on the front door, followed by Jed calling her name. Wondering who it could be, she quickly wiped her hands on her apron and rushed into the den. A curious Lulu and Bernita trailed closely behind her. Her mouth flew open in surprise when she saw Clarence crouched in the doorway in his bib overalls and holding his straw hat in his hands.

"Clarence, how are you?" It was only three days ago when she met him at the dance. She was thrilled he came to visit her like he promised.

"I hope this isn't a bad time," he said. "I happen to be down this way. Thought I might stop by and see if you could take my company."

She grabbed his hand and pulled him into the room. "No. This is a better time than any. Come on in and meet my brother and sisters. This is Jed," she said gesturing to him.

"Howdy do," Jed said.

"And this here is Lulu." She wrapped her arms around her. "Sometimes we call her little Lulu. And you met Berni…" Maggie began as she turned around. "Oh, where did Bernita go? She was right behind me." She shrugged her shoulders and said, "Ma and Pa are out back in the herb garden. I'll take you to meet them."

After introducing Clarence to her parents, Maggie led him to the wrought-iron swing under a large shade tree in the front yard near where he tethered his horse-drawn wagon.

Her parents had a lot of questions for him when he asked permission to court her; they wanted to know where he lived, what he did for a living, all about his parents and relatives, and where he attended church. Maggie could tell Clarence was nervous by the way he kept shifting from side to side and fidgeting. She was relieved when the ordeal ended for him, and they gave their approval.

"Your parents are nice," Clarence said as he reached down to pat the mutt that sniffed at his legs. "I like that little herb garden they got out back."

It's Ma's pride and joy."

Last year her father made a half enclosed screened covering behind the house for her mother to cultivate the herbs she scavenged in the woods, riverbanks, and fields. From skills passed down from her grandmother and great grandmother, Maggie's mother knew how to make a variety of concoctions and poultices to use on ailments ranging from sore throats, colds, insect bites and belly aches, to cuts and wounds. Maggie's favorite herb was the peppermint. A soothing tea made with the leaves always gave her relief when she had an upset stomach.

"I couldn't ask for better parents. They worked so hard for us to have a better life. But I worry about them sometimes."

Clarence started the swing in motion with a push of his foot. "Well, at least they got their own land to farm instead of having to work someone else's. That's saying a lot."

"Are y'all sharecroppers?"

"Yeah. Down on the Davis place." Clarence looked across the big, dirt yard to the large garden several feet away. "My Pa hopes to farm his own land one of these days, too."

"He got any land in mind?"

"Yep. About thirty acres or so."

"That's good. Y'all getting it soon?"

"Naw. Not ready yet. Right now, we are doing all we can to scrape and save every penny we get our hands on. Times kind of hard these days. Cotton not going for much on the market."

"Things haven't been going too well on the farm for us either. Pa says it's the depression the country is going through. Folks just don't have the money to spend."

Clarence ran a hand over his head. "I'm sure hoping things will get better soon."

"Me too," Maggie agreed. "I had thoughts of going up north to find work to help my folks out. I hear there are good paying jobs up there."

"That's so?" Clarence said inquisitively.

"That's what I heard. My parents are against it though, so I guess I just have to get it out of my head."

Brushing a strand of flyaway hair from her face, he said gently, "Well, I know a person got to do what they got to do to survive, but surely my luck can't be that bad."

Maggie turned to face him. "What you mean?"

He gave her a lopsided grin. "I finally meet the girl of my dreams and then she ups and moves miles away. I call that bad luck."

Maggie beamed. It made her feel content that Clarence considered her the girl of his dreams and no doubt in her mind she felt she finally found the person of her dreams. "I'm glad you stopped by to see me," she said in a soft voice.

Clarence gazed at her fondly. "Didn't want to pass up the opportunity to visit a pretty lady."

Maggie suddenly felt self-conscious. She wasn't used to men like him. She picked at a spot on her dress. Her previous suitors always acted nervous around her, not sure of what to say or how to act. Clarence was different. Although he had a quiet demeanor, he didn't lack confidence. He knew all the right words to say. His charm drew her in to him and stirred her interest.

"When I first laid eyes on you at the dance," Clarence continued, "I knew I wanted to know more about you. I feel blessed to have met a woman as kind and beautiful as you."

"Thank you, Clarence."

"I'm glad your Ma and Pa said I could court you but you sure there isn't someone special in your life already?"

"I'm very sure. Why you ask?"

"Because I don't want to have to fight off competition."

Maggie threw her head back and laughed. "Well, there's no one else. I promise."

She laughed louder when Clarence breathed a mock sigh of relief and wiped his forehead of pretend sweat.

In a more serious tone of voice, he said, "I want to be that special someone in your life." He locked eyes with hers and reached for her hand.

Maggie bit her lower lip and became lost in his smothering, brown eyes. They sat in silence, hand in hand, enjoying the gentle, relaxing motion of the swing and their blissful moment together.

The approaching pit-pat of bare feet running on the hard, bare earth, broke the spell between them.

"Ma says for me to come out and sit with y'all," Lulu said before wiggling in between them on the swing.

Heat rushed to Maggie's face. She quickly untwined her fingers from Clarence. "My folks are so old-fashioned," she said apologetically. "It's against their rules for us girls to be alone in the company of a male."

"Don't worry about that none. Whenever my sisters have suitors come to visit, my Ma sits within earshot."

Maggie laughed. "Mine plants herself right down in the den pretending that she's not paying us no mind while all the time her ears are flopped wide open."

"With that being said, I don't want to start off on the wrong foot. I guess it best I be heading on. It'll be getting dark soon, anyway," Clarence said as he stood up. "Think I can visit you again Sunday?"

"Sunday is fine."

Maggie followed Clarence to his wagon and watched him start down the long, dirt path to the main road. When he was halfway, he turned and waved. When she could no longer see him, she grabbed Lulu's hand and skipped to the house.

***

Later that evening, Maggie hummed an upbeat tune to a song while helping Bernita snap beans in the kitchen.

"Why you so happy?" Bernita asked nonchalantly. But she knew the answer already.

"I can't believe it. Clarence kept his promise and came to visit me. We gonna start courting." Maggie gave Bernita a long look and cocked her head to one side. "Where you run off to?"

"I had things to do," she replied curtly. "Clarence coming to see you aint no big deal."

"It's a big deal to me. He's so sweet. You should have at least stuck around to speak to him. That was so rude of you. Don't you think?"

"Hump," Bernita grunted. Why should she have stayed? She thought to herself. To have it rubbed in her face? She wanted to tell Maggie the truth. That she had hoped it could've been her that Clarence was coming to visit but she kept it to herself. When she had followed Maggie into the living room and saw him standing there, her heart dropped yet again. He wasn't coming to visit her. It was more than she could stand.

She had left the room and retreated into the kitchen. With her ear glued to the kitchen door, she could hear Maggie in her sickly, sweet voice gushing all over him. Feeling devastated, she didn't come out until she knew they were outside.

"Maggie got a boyfriend," Lulu's voice rang out as Bernita bounded up the stairs leading to the bedroom. "And he handsome," she added.

Bernita stopped and scowled at her. "He got buckteeth."

"No, he don't," Lulu said emphatically. "You just jealous cause no boys come to court you."

"Shut up, big mouth," Bernita spat out, then ran up the stairs before Lulu could say anything else.

She sat on the straw, tick bed in the narrow room and peered longingly out the window. She watched as Maggie lead Clarence through the front yard and laughing occasionally at whatever he was saying. Bernita couldn't help but notice the tender and affectionate way Clarence looked at her. She watched them a few moments more, then, feeling miserable, she closed the shutters to the window, so she wouldn't have to see them any longer.

"Don't you think so?"

Maggie's question penetrated through the fog in Bernita's mind. "Think what?" She snapped in irritation.

"Rude!"

The nerve of Maggie calling her rude. She had a question of her own to ask. "Why did you throw yourself all over him at the dance? Don't you think that was rude?" she replied indignantly.

"I didn't throw myself at him. I acted like a perfect lady. That's more than I can say for you. If you stopped being such a wild tomboy maybe more boys might be interested in you."

"Everybody saw how you were a carrying on," Bernita retorted as she snapped a bean into thirds. "You threw yourself at him."

"He asked me for a dance, Bernita. I said 'of course, I would love too,' Maggie said extending her hand out with emphasis. "I did not throw myself at him by no means."

"A lot of girls are after him, you know?"

"Well, I don't have to worry about other girls". Maggie said with self-assuredness. "Clarence wants me to be his girl."

Maggie's smugness infuriated her. Hump, Bernita thought, you a fool if you think Clarence is all yours. There might be a girl out there who'll take him away from you. And I just might be that girl. After all, all's fair in love and war they say. One day Clarence will come to his senses and choose me.

5

Clarence whistled gayly as he geared his horse along a lonely, shadowed country road. He left Maggie's house feeling like the happiest man in the world. Although it was the middle of the week, he was glad he made the bold decision to head down the road to her house after he had finished with his errands. He was hesitant at first because most women took company on Sundays. The weekdays were set aside for their chores. But he had an urgent need to see her. He wanted to court her and needed to make sure she was really interested in him and not just something he imagined in his head.

To his relief the visit went well. He had been nervous under her parents' interrogations, but he must have said the right words. He passed their test, and they gave him permission to court their daughter. Once alone with Maggie he felt at ease. Although surprised, he was pleased when she said she wasn't courting anyone. A pretty girl like her always had all kinds of men lined up at her doorsteps like hungry wolves. Lucky for him there were no other suitors.

He smiled as his thoughts led back to the dance. He had mustered up enough nerves to walk up to her expecting to be turned down flat. From experience he knew beautiful girls could be stuck on themselves. Most of them wouldn't give a man like him the time of day. He wasn't dressed dapper and didn't talk slick like some of the men at the dance. Those were the type of men who usually got all the attention from the females. But Maggie proved to be cut from a different mold. She wasn't like those other girls.

Clarence skillfully guided the horse around a curve in the road as he let Saturday night replay in his mind. He wasn't particularly fond of dances, and in fact he hadn't planned on going. His cousin had been insistent though and refused to take no for an answer. He convinced him he needed to get out more if he had hopes of ever finding a wife one day.

He wouldn't find what he was looking for in the fields and woods where he spent most of his time. He knew his cousin was right. Most of the free moments were spent hunting and fishing. It was high time for him to move out of his parents' home and settle down in his own place and raise a family.

He had courted a few women in the past who were more than eager to get married, but he wasn't making enough money to build a life with a family. They would have only ended up etching out a life in poverty and he refused to put a family of his through such hardships. It wasn't easy to not have much to show for himself.

Women didn't understand the pride of a man. A man wanted to care, protect, and provide otherwise they felt disgraced and shamed when they couldn't meet those needs.

With his finances improving he was now ready to take that plunge. His future was looking brighter. He only had to find the right partner willing to take the plunge with him and build a bright future together.

He went to the dance with no expectations and was pleasantly surprised at the number of unattached young ladies there. Although he had his pick of women that night, only one caught his eye.

Clarence maneuvered the wagon down a narrow, crooked trail through a wooded area thick with underbrush and came upon a tiny shack of a house. An elderly man and woman were standing in the yard over a large, black pot. A low fire underneath the pot sent gray smoke spiraling upwards. The lady stuck a large stick in the pot and stirred the contents in it.

"Hey, Grandmama. Hey Grandpa."

"What ya know thar son," his grandfather called back.

Clarence brought the wagon to a stop. "What's in the pot?"

"Got us four rabbits," his grandmother called out.

He thought so. He could smell the gamy odor as soon as he turned down the trail.

"Ya welcome to come back and get you some grub after you get yo'self settled."

"Okay, grandmama. I'll be back around." Clarence continued around the house down another narrow trail.

His folks lived on the same sharecropper property several yards behind his grandparents in a similar style shack; a crude tin roof, three-room hut with a loft. There was no indoor plumbing or kitchen. He continued down the trail, thinking to himself that he's finally found his future bride. One day, he would have to bring Maggie to meet his parents and grandparents. He just hoped their dire poverty wouldn't be a shock to her. Her family seemed to be a notch or two higher on the ladder than his. He made a vow to purchase his own land as soon as he could and build her a house worthy for her to call home.

6

Clarence courted Maggie regularly after that first visit, and by the end of June, he was practically part of the family. Initially, he visited her on Sunday afternoons. Sometimes he would come over early on Sunday mornings in his wagon to go to church with her. The older women in the congregation gushed over him with mock flirtations. Clarence in return indulged them with compliments, enduring them to vie for his attention. The attention the women showered on Clarence amused her. She knew he was a good catch, and she was proud to show him off.

Clarence exuded all the right qualities she ever hoped for in a man. She not only liked his affectionate nature and sense of humor, but she also admired his dedicated ambition. He didn't mind hard work. Whenever he had time away from his work in the fields, he would come over to help them with their farming. He refused to accept any pay. Jed playfully teased Maggie that Clarence only wanted to get in good with their father. In which she reminded him that he benefitted as well from having the extra help. It meant less work for him. The reminder usually shut Jed up for the time being.

Maggie knew her father welcomed having Clarence helping on the farm. Besides, she also knew that there was way too much on his mind to take stock in any hidden agenda he might have. The first crop of beans and corn had been plentiful, but they didn't sell well at the market. The mortgage on the farm was already two months overdue. To make matters worse, a powerful storm in the middle of June, with hail the size of crab apples, nearly wiped out the second crop of beans.

Although her parents tried to keep their financial problems away from the children, Maggie overheard them talking one night. They feared losing the farm and everything they had worked so hard for if their luck continued to spiral downwards. The seriousness of the implications concerned her. Too much hard work and labor had been put into the farm to keep it running. Her father was a proud man; to be able to work for himself and be out from under the system of sharecropping was something he was the proudest of. It would be a shame to lose it all. The effects of the mental toil and stress on him was obvious to Maggie. She could only pray for things to get better.

One hot day in early July, Maggie led Clarence out back to where a large oak tree provided shade from the summer heat. They sat alone for a change on the wooden steps of the porch. She was glad Clarence had proven his trustworthiness to her parents. Her mother began to let up on chaperoning whenever he came to court her.

"Dinner sho was good. Boy, am I stuffed," Clarence said, rubbing his belly as he leaned backward on the steps. "You Smith women know how to cook."

Maggie laughed at the sight of him poking out his stomach and rubbing his hands across it. "What you like best?" she asked between chuckles.

"If I must choose, I got to say the peach cobbler. The best I ever ate."

"Good. That's what I whipped up."

Lulu stuck her head out from around the big honeysuckle bush at the side of the house. "I cooked the biscuits," she said proudly.

Startled, Maggie looked around just in time to see Lulu duck back behind the bush. They weren't as alone as she had thought.

"You did?" Clarence called. "Those were some mighty good-tasting biscuits. I must of eaten at least five or six of them myself."

Lulu giggled from behind the bush.

"Lulu, what in heaven's name are you doing hiding over there? Run and play before I call Ma."

Sticking her head out again she asked, "Are you and Clarence gonna kiss?"

Irritated, Maggie stood up and started toward the honeysuckle bush. "Go and play somewhere else, Lulu, and stop being so nosy. Go on now."

Lulu jumped up from her hiding place and ran off, giggling.

Maggie rejoined Clarence on the steps, thinking they could now enjoy their quiet time together when Buster came from around the other side of the house. "Want to play stickball with me and Jed, Clarence?"

"Not this time sport, catch me on another day," Clarence said, rising from his reclining position.

Maggie rolled her eyes upward and sighed. "There's no privacy around here. Let's go for a walk."

"You sure it'll be all right?" he asked.

"Yeah. I'm sure." Then to Buster she said, "Tell Ma me and Clarence going for a stroll to walk off supper."

She sauntered out of the yard hand in hand with Clarence, heading down the long narrow, dirt path. On either side of them were fields of ankle-deep turfs of green grass interspersed with tall yellow and beige switchgrass. Yellow passion flowers, goldenrods, daisies, and violet wisteria flowed gracefully throughout the field.

The splendor of the blossoms seemed to stand out more than ever to her. The swift flight of butterflies looking for sweet nectar and the sensuous smell in the air along with the brilliance of the flowery meadows enchanted her. Strolling down the ordinary trail, one she'd walked over a thousand times before, was now magically transformed with him by her side. It was such an enthralling moment that she became giddy with happiness.

Clarence stopped to pick a handful of the yellow, purple, and white blooms and presented them to her.

The romantic gesture pleased her. "Mmm. Nice. Thank you," she said. "They're beautiful."

Then, in one swift motion, he reached behind her head and undid the lavender ribbon around her ponytail. He tied the flowers together in a bouquet and handed them to her. "There. A perfect bouquet for a perfect lady."

They continued their stroll, enjoying their special alone time together. When they were a considerable distance away from the house with no chance of being interrupted, Maggie gave Clarence a playful shove then ran through the meadows holding the bouquet tight in her hands.

As if on cue, he pursued in the chase, but her long, agile legs almost proved too much for him. When he caught up with her, they both collapsed to the ground under the thick canopy of a large, thirty-foot tall, weeping willow tree with long, pliant limbs hanging to the ground.

"Got ya," Clarence said, grabbing her by the waist. He began tickling her ribs.

Maggie giggled and writhed around on the ground, trying to get away from the pleasant torture. "Okay! Okay! Stop!" she spurted out in between laughter. "Don't tickle me anymore!"

"You promise not to run again?"

"I promise."

He stopped tickling her but kept his hands on her tiny waist. "Say 'I swear'," he commanded.

"I don't swear," Maggie said self-righteously. When his hands went toward her ribs she quickly said, "I swear. I swear."

"That's more like it." He rolled onto his back, breathing heavy.

Also out of breath, Maggie slid closer to him and rested her head on his shoulder. She lay watching the rising and falling of his chest, and then glimpsed through the dainty branches of the willow white fluffy clouds floating lazily across the blue sky. Maggie let out a sigh. If only this moment could last forever, she thought to herself.

Turning to face her he said, "We been courting for a while now. Going on three months."

Maggie brushed a speck of grass out of his hair. "It seems like I've known you forever." She meant what she said. Clarence had become such a big part of her now that it felt like he's always been around. She couldn't imagine her life without him. They belonged together. Not only had he become intertwined in her family, but she also fell in love with his family when he finally took her to meet them, especially his grandparents who were sweet to her.

Clarence had sheepishly apologized before taking her to his homeplace about the poor condition of how they lived. He had seemed embarrassed about their sharecropper shanty, but she assured him that they were basically in the same boat. Her father had just got lucky enough to buy his own land, and Clarence's father had the same aspirations for himself.

He stroked her cheek tenderly, then brought his face closer to hers, causing her skin to tingle with anticipation.

"I love you, Maggie Smith."

She looked deep into his eyes. "I love you, too, Clarence Westbrook."

A strong passion rose within her. Clarence pulled her closer to him. They wrapped their arms around each other until their bodies merged. He kissed her on her forehead, the tip of her nose, then found her mouth. With a tilt of his head, he brushed his warm, soft lips gently to hers and drew her upper lip into his mouth.

A fluttery feeling rose in her stomach as if butterflies were flapping around inside. He was stirring feelings she had never experienced before. She parted her lips and returned his kiss. In an instant their tongues were circling in an exotic dance. It wasn't their first kiss, but the first kiss that conjured up such deep passion in her.

After a moment, Clarence disengaged his lips from hers but still held her close. He whispered in her ear, "I won't let anything come between the love I have for you. Can you promise me the same, Maggie?"

"I promise," she said before melting into his arms again to seek his soft lips. The gentle caresses on her back were inviting, but when his hand slid toward her buttock, she reluctantly pulled loose from his eager mouth. Her mother had instilled in her the virtues and pitfalls of not giving in before marriage.

She feared if she laid on the ground with Clarence an instant longer, she risked losing herself in the rising waves of his kisses forever. "We best head on back to the house before Ma send Lulu looking for us," she said as she tried to control her heavy breathing.

Once back on their feet they helped each other wipe off any tell-tell signs of grass on their clothing.

After that day the willow tree became Maggie's and Clarence special, secret place to be alone whenever they could slip away. Their own private shelter sitting on a mound of a hill near a creek, out of sight of nosey siblings. Under the weeping willow, they held each other tight, shared their hopes and dreams, and pretended that the world was perfect if only for the brief time they were together.

Maggie looked forward to the cherished moments spent with him. He had awakened in her desires she didn't know she had. Being the gentleman that he was, however, he never let his hands wander further than she would allow. The more time she spent with him, Philadelphia receded further and further to the back of her mind. True love had taken over.

7

"Want some cool, fresh water, Clarence?" Bernita cooed as soon as Clarence walked into the yard with Jed. They had been working in the field all morning and was taking their mid-day break. She dipped the long-handled dipper into the bucket of water she drew from the well and held it out to him.

"I'll take a sip," Jed said and took the dipper from her hand.

Bernita glared at him. "I asked Clarence. Not you!"

Jed took a big gulp and handed the dipper back to her. "I'm going round back."

"I'll join you in a minute after I wet my whistle," Clarence said.

Bernita breathed a sigh of relief. It's about time I get him all to myself. "Here, I know you must be awfully tired," she said sweetly after dipping out some more water.

"Thanks. My throat as dry as a rock."

She watched him arch his head back and guzzle the cool liquid down his throat. The way his Adam's Apple bobbled with each swallow fascinated her. Her eyes traveled slowly down from his muscled shoulders that glistened with the sweat of his morning labor to his thick, firm biceps. Bernita flicked her tongue across her lower lip. "I can tell you're a hard worker."

He wiped his arm across his mouth. "Yeah? How's that?" He responded with amusement.

Bernita squeezed a bulging bicep as he brought the dipper back to his mouth, "Strong arms. I bet you could wrestle a bear."

Clarence grinned. "You think so, huh?"

"Yep. I do." Bernita murmured as she visioned those powerful arms wrapped round her.

She was gaping at him with admiration, when out the corner of her eye, she spotted her mother coming around the corner of the house carrying a big bucket of fertilizer.

"Hey, Mrs. Smith," Clarence called out. "Need some help with that?"

"I reckon I could," she called back.

Annoyance crossed Bernita's face despite her efforts to hide it. Damn it. Why did her Ma have to pick this time of all times to come out to work in her stupid garden? Just when she had Clarence's full attention for a change.

Seemed that no matter how hard she tried to lure him her way nothing worked. It just wasn't an easy thing to do with her sister around all the time. What was it going to take to get him to court her instead of Maggie, she wondered? It hurt to see them walking in the yard holding hands or sitting cozy on the swing. Maggie could have anyone she wanted but she was always gloating and carrying on about Clarence. She was so sure of herself. Well, she wanted Clarence. She saw him first, and, so far, the battle wasn't over yet.

Bernita watched with yearning as Clarence snatched clumps of wild Bermuda grass from around the petunias before she carried the bucket of water into the house.

8

Maggie woke up at five o'clock Saturday morning feeling perky and jubilant. She bounced out of bed and peeked out the window to see that the pounding rain through the night had finally stopped. Today is going to be perfect, she thought to herself.

Her father promised them they could ride into town with him to deliver vegetables to the general store and she was excited. The whole family looked forward to the luxury of the monthly trip into town. It was fifteen miles away by wagon, and her father liked to get a good head start before the sun got too high in the sky. That meant all their chores had to be done before they left.

Gently nudging Lulu, she said, "Get up, sleepy head."

Lulu opened her big brown eyes and gave her a blank stare.

"We best get moving if we want to go with Pa into town," Maggie urged.

Lulu stretched her arms, rubbed her eyes, then slid her feet to the floor.

She looked over at Bernita, sleeping soundly. Waking her would not be as easy. "Get up, Bernita!" Maggie said in a loud voice. She gave her a firm shake. When that didn't work, she tried another tactic and pulled off the heavy quilt, exposing her to the stark chilliness of the room.

"Leave me alone," Bernita grumbled, reaching down to retrieve the cover.

"We have to get going if we want to go with Pa into town."

Bernita sat bolt upright at the mention of town.

Bernita loved going to town more than any of them. Trouble seemed to follow her though wherever she went. She always managed to get herself into some sort of mishap. A couple of years ago, she and two of her rowdy friends got into a rock fight with some boys and a store window ended up broken.

Her father, along with the father of the two other girls, had to pitch in to replace it. He was so angry at Bernita that he threatened not to take any of them into town with him anymore.

Thankfully, her mother came to the rescue and persuaded him not to take Bernita's foolishness out on the rest of the children, since they weren't involved. Bernita ended up getting the full punishment. She couldn't go to town with the rest of the family for three months, plus she had to do extra chores around the house. As usual, Bernita resorted to her childish ways and tried throwing her hissy fits, but it didn't work. Her parents stood their ground and turned a deaf ear to teach her a lesson.

Maggie hoped Bernita learned her lesson well and would behave herself on this trip, but she wasn't going to waste her time worrying about her. Happier thoughts were on her mind. Clarence planned to meet her downtown as soon as he finished his work.

Satisfied that Bernita was now wide awake, her next mission was the alcove on the other side of the loft where Buster slept. Jed was already up and dressed and downstairs helping their father load up the wagon.

***

Jed and Lulu sat on the front seat with their father. Maggie sat in the back of the wagon with Bernita and Buster and the crates of produce. Her mother planned on spending the day with her sick aunt and didn't go with them this trip.

The wagon bumped along for two miles on a hardened dirt road, pocketed with muddy ruts, until it reached the main road leading into town. Maggie didn't mind the jarring ride. Thanks to the rain last night, the air felt cool and refreshing on her skin. She leaned against a crate and enjoyed the scenery.

Watching miles and miles of cotton fields and pastures full of cows roll by put her in a peaceful mood. Occasionally, a house came into view in between massive farmland. The homes, with its gleaming, white colonial columns and immaculate lawns, brought to her mind of how her grandparents slaved in those very same fields, picking cotton in sweltering heat and suffering all sorts of abuse. The big houses contrasted with the tin-roofed shanties and shacks of sharecroppers hidden behind clusters of trees or out in open clearings.

Hoop county was a rural area about two hundred miles from the nearest big city in South Carolina. Maggie learned from her history studies, in the one room school she attended up to seventh grade, that a Scotsman, Daniel Hooper, established the township of Hoop County in the 1830s. He had come down from Ohio looking for fertile land to invest in. He bought over a thousand acres and built a large cotton empire and owned a total of a hundred slaves. The union soldiers burned his plantation to the ground during the civil war. Afterwards, he sold parcels of his property to the overseers who worked for him and moved back to Ohio with his fortunes.

The County didn't flourish with industries and factories after the war like most of the larger towns in South Carolina. In fact, there were only two factories in the area. It was a poor County that saw meager progress over the years. Farming was the livelihood most people, colored and white, depended on.

Maggie' father guided the mule into town taking care to dodge people roaming up and down the street on their weekly shopping errands. The town was less than three miles long and only a quarter of a mile wide. Most of the street was paved with cobblestone except the last portion near the end of town which was hard packed dirt and gravel. Only a few cars dotted parking spaces. Most people, not able to afford such a luxury, came to town in wagons or on horseback.

Mr. Smith found a hitching post in the alley near the general store and announced, "Alrighty, we made it."

Jed jumped out of the wagon and tethered the horse.

Buster and Lulu let out yelps and whoops as they scampered off the wagon and made a dash for the store.

Mr. Smith called out to them, "Don't y'all be a playing around in there breaking nothing. ya hear?"

With one swift jump, Bernita was right behind Lulu and Buster. Maggie tucked her dress between her knees and gingerly put one foot over the rail, then the other until she was standing on firm ground.

9

The modest, well-stocked, dimly lit store smelt of a mixture of animal feed, spices, fresh produce, and hot dogs. Starting near the front of the store, lining down the middle were crates and barrels filled with an assortment of vegetables and staples such as flour, meal, sugar, rice, and grits.

On one side of the store, tin cooking utensils took up space on shelves alongside canned food, household items and mason jars. Farming tools hung on the wall on the opposite side. Just about anything necessary for country living could be found in the little store.

Maggie wandered around while her father bargained with Mr. Hendrix on a price for his three bushels of corn, two bushels of beans and ten heads of cabbage. A bundle of pink, floral material in the back, near a haphazard stack of seeds caught her attention. Maggie stroked the soft cotton. Her father had warned them before leaving the house not to ask for anything extra, so she made a mental note to save up enough of the money she earned from helping her mother as a washer woman to buy a yard of it on her next trip.

Up front at the counter, the store owner opened the cash register and counted out three dollars.

"I thank ya, Mr. Hendrix," Maggie heard her father saying. "I was hoping for a little more, but I do appreciate whatever I can get."

"Sorry, Silas. That's all I can give you. You know how things are these days."

"Yes sir. I sure do."

Maggie' father had been dealing with Mr. Hendrix for several years, forming an amicable relationship. Most of the colored and whites were acquainted with each other in Hoop County. The colored folks knew, though, that there was a thin line not to cross. Even if they were older than a white person it was expected of them to be submissive and to stay in their place. Lynching and night riders didn't take place but there was news of it taking place in neighboring counties and it lurked just beneath the surface in Hoop County.

"You need to stock up on anything whiles you here?" the store owner asked.

Mr. Smith took a scrap of paper out of his pocket with a list of items scribbled on it from his wife. "Let's see, how about a box of salt, a pound of sugar, five pounds of cornmeal and five pounds of grits."

"Coming right up." Mr. Hendrix grabbed some brown, waxed paper bags and came from around the counter.

Mr. Smith followed him to the middle of the store to a barrel where he began scooping up cornmeal.

"How the farming coming along?" Mr. Hendrix asked.

"Been pretty rough. Lost most my corn in the flood. I'm just managing to stay afloat by the grace of God."

The store owner shook his head from side to side. "The worst flood in these parts in years. It plum near wiped out old man Nelson's field."

"You don't say? I guess us poor farmers jus' don't stand a chance sometimes. Not much we can do but lick our wounds and keep on a plowing."

"You right about that, Silas. I just hope that New Deal Program and that thar farm bill President Roosevelt got started will help the farmers out. I heard on the radio farmers everywhere going bankrupt and losing their lands."

"I'm a praying real hard that won't be my luck, Mr. Hendrix, but between nature, them bankers and those new, big, shiny tractors some of them wealthy farmers using these days, I could very well end up in the same boat.

"Hang on in thar you hear. Don't you give up too soon."

"I ain't intending to do that. I got mouths to feed."

After Mr. Hendrix finished measuring out the meal, sugar, salt, and grits, Mr. Smith followed him back to the cash register where he had him throw in six hot dogs and six salted nut rolls. From the soda machine out front he bought three drinks for them to share. Buster and Jed split a Mountain Dew, Bernita and Lulu split an Orange Crush, and Maggie split a Royal Crown with her father. Maggie came out on the lucky end because her father wasn't much of a soda drinker.

Drinks, hot dogs, and candy bars finished they were off to explore on their own. Mr. Smith sat on the porch of the store in one of the rocking chairs to talk politics and farming with three other men. He gave Bernita and Maggie strict instructions, since they were the oldest, to keep a watchful eye out for their two younger siblings. Jed and Buster ran across the street to the depot to watch for incoming trains. Lulu played hopscotch in front of the store with a white girl around her age.

Before Maggie could ask Bernita which way she wanted to go Bernita had taken off across the street, prancing down the sidewalk as if she didn't have a care in the world. In the past they would have put their differences aside when they came to town and explored the shops together. But lately, Bernita had been acting angry and hostile towards her, and she didn't have a clue as to why. She followed Bernita with her eyes for a moment, shrugged her shoulders, then wandered down the sidewalk to window shop alone.

Maggie noticed new stores had cropped up downtown since their last visit. There were a Western Auto, a Sears & Roebuck and construction was going on for a Belk's at the end of North Main. She poked around inside a lady's boutique store nestled between a clock repair shop and a paint supply store for a few minutes to check out the latest style, then continued her journey, proceeding cautiously around the construction site of an A & P grocery store. Although glad to see a major grocery store coming to town, she hoped Mr. Hendrix' general store wouldn't be put out of business. It had been around forever, and she loved its quaintness.

Pausing at a nickel and dime store, she scanned an exhibition of cosmetics stacked in the window. Cold cream, lipsticks, face powder, nail polishes, eye shadows and rogue were expertly displayed. A poster of a white lady dressed in an elegant red evening gown, with one leg peeking out through a long slit, stood in the opposite window. Beneath it an advertisement read, 'Pure Silk Hosiery of Lustrous Beauty and Fine Texture.' She studied the poster, wondering what the smooth feel of silk against her skin instead of the hot, rough, cotton hose she had to wear to church would feel like.

Walking a few more blocks led her to Sears. Maggie put her face up to the window and cupped her hands along the side of her head to peer inside. Squinting, she read the tag on a wringer washing machine. Fifty-nine dollars and ninety-five cents. Eight dollars down. Two dollars a month. Her mind was lost in thought as she daydreamed of how much easier her mother's life would be with a real washing machine when suddenly, two hands landed on top of her shoulders. She jumped and whirled around. Her eye, wide with fright, became narrow as her brows creased into angry furrows when she saw the person behind her.

"Clarence! You scared the devil out of me!"

"Sorry about that, "Clarence said with a chuckle. "How's my girl this lovely day?"

"I'm fine," Maggie said with a pout. "I'm mad at you though, for sneaking up on me like that." Clarence laughed.

"And it not funny! I could have peed myself!" She balled up a fist and swung it at him.

He ducked her fist and laughed, "Hey, be careful. One of those mean punches might land on the target." Clarence suddenly pulled Maggie closer to him and surprised her with a light kiss on her lips.

She quickly pushed him away. "Clarence! My father might be watching." She said as she glanced down the street toward the general store.

"I'm just glad to see my sweetheart." He stepped back and looked down the street. "He can't see us this far away anyway."

"I saw y'all," an accusing voice behind her announced.

Maggie turned around to face Bernita standing with her hands on her hips scowling at her. Her friend Rosa stood beside with a smirk on her face.

Bernita crinkled her nose. "Wait till Ma find out you was a kissing Clarence like some floozy," she said with smug satisfaction.

"I was not!," Maggie objected. "Stop sticking your nose where it don't belong."

"Hey, Bernita," Clarence said jovially. "It was the other way 'round. I kissed her. I guess that makes me a loose man," he said with a laugh.

Tickled by his sense of humor, Maggie laughed along with him.

Bernita looked from Clarence to Maggie and back to Clarence with disdain, then said, "Come on, Rosa." She took off in a huff with Rosa trailing behind her.

"What's eating her?" Clarence asked.

"Who knows?" Maggie said as she watched Bonita and Rosa walk away. "She's just have a mean rebellious spirit."

"Well, y'all as different as night and day that's for sure. Glad I got the sister with the sweet attitude," he said as he wrapped an arm around her and gave her a squeeze. "Come on I'll buy you an ice-cream cone."

They joined hands and strolled to the Ice Cream parlor a block away.

***

"So, Clarence been courting Maggie a lot, huh?" Rosa asked. They were leaning up against a white picket fence at the edge of town.

Bernita lips turned downwards, "Yeah. He always at the house."

"Seem like he's really in love with her," Rosa said.

A wistful look spread across Bernita's face as she sucked on a red lollipop. "It should be me," she in a low voice, unaware that her murmur was loud enough to hear.

"Might as well get that out your mind. He's smitten by Maggie. I can tell."

"He's under her spell for sure," she said throwing the lollipop into the grass as if it suddenly had a bitter taste.

"Hey, I got an idea," Rosa said with excitement. "Why don't we go see Miss. Hortense to get one of her love portions. You put one of those on him, next thing you know he a be swooning all over you."

"I don't believe in that silly stuff."

"Mildred says that's how she got Tucker."

Bernita looked at her in disbelief. "With a love portion?"

"Uh huh, sure did. She swears by Miss Hortense roots. She says it works. What you need to do is to get a bit of his hair and…"

"Even if that crazy mess work, I want to hook my man with my own magic. I don't need Miss Hortense," Bernita said, cutting her off before she could finish.

"Your magic ain't been working so far," Rosa said with a laugh.

Bernita creased her brows and folded her arms across her chest. "It will take time. It's as if Maggie really do have him under her spell or something."

"You think she went to see Miss. Hortense?"

"Don't be silly. Maggie never needed help to get a man interested in her."

"Yep, you right about that." Then in a loud voice said, "Well, speak of the devil!"

Bernita watched as Maggie crossed the street and headed in their direction.

"It's time to get back to the wagon," she called out as she approached them.

"We still got plenty of time," Bernita said, although she was aware their four hours in town were up for the day.

"You should come on now, so you don't keep Pa waiting."

"Did he send you to get me?"

"No. But..."

"You're so bossy," Rosa said. "If Clarence knew just how bossy you really is, he would drop you faster than a bird flying out of a cat's mouth."

Maggie pursed her mouth to reply to Rosa, but too flustered to speak, she instead turned around and walked away.

10

"There, that ought to do it. See how it a working now, Jed,"
Mr. Smith said, stepping back to now, Jed," Mr. Smith said,
stepping back to now, Jed," Mr. Smith said, stepping back
to examine the barn door. A heavy wind blew the door off
its hinges in the night because it wasn't latched properly. He
and Jed had gotten up early to tackle it before tackling their
other chores for the day.

The barn was in the back of the house down a narrow
trail about two hundred feet away. A field of corn and beans
spread out behind it. The cow pasture framed one side of
the barn and the pig pen sat a few feet away on the other
side.

Maggie headed down the trail toward the barn with a
milk pail in her hand. She paused at the entrance to watch
her father and brother busy at work on their project.

The door squeaked each time Jed opened and closed it.
"Seems good as new," he said. "Tho, it could use a little
more oil I guess."

"Sounds to me that door need a whole lot more oil," Maggie said, teasing him. She then called out, "Good morning, y'all."

Jed, joking back, said, "Nobody asked for your two cents. I'll go get the oil, Pa."

Maggie went inside the barn and grabbed the milking stool. "Hold on now, Betsy. Time to be milked," she said to the jittery cow. "I.m not liking this no more than you."

After thoroughly washing the cow's udders she squeezed them in succession until milk squirted out into the pail with a pattering sound against the tin. She did the milking in the early wee hours of the morning and again at dusk. Usually, no one else was up except her mother, father, and Jed. She welcomed the morning solitude, and the soothing sounds of the farm as it came awake.

The barn door creaked open, and Maggie tilted her head around the stall to see her father coming toward her.

"Got that door finished yet, Pa?" she called out as she skillfully aimed milk into the pail.

"Just bout. How thangs going with you and Clarence?"

His blunt question surprised her. He wasn't one to meddle too much in her social life. Her mother kept on top of what went on with the girls. "Good, Pa," she answered.

"Y'all planning on getting hitched soon?"

Maggie stopped milking and looked around at him, not sure where the conversation was heading. "Why you ask?"

"Well, are y'all?" he asked bluntly.

"We talked' bout it.

"He a fine young man. A good hard worker. Wouldn't blame ya none if ya'll jumped the broom and tied the knot."

"The time isn't right for us. He wants to save up to buy some land. So, it might be another year or so."

"In that case me and your Ma had a talk last night about you going up north. We decided to let you go."

Maggie's mouth flew wide open in surprise.

"We got a letter from Rick yesterday. He said the place where Daisy work plans on hiring ten people in October."

She was so shocked by the good news that all she could do was just stare at her father speechless.

"Daisy told her supervisor to put in a word for you being that you a good seamstress and all. She said they could use you. So... if you still want to go..."

Before he could finish his sentence, Maggie jumped up to hug him almost knocking the pail of milk over in the process. "I still want to go! Thanks, Pa! I will send money home to help you and Ma out."

"Lord knows it will be a big help having the extra income coming in. Course we don't expect you to be gone no longer than a year. By the time you come back Clarence should be ready to be your husband and you his wife."

Happy beyond belief, Maggie said, "I promise to make you so proud of me, Pa."

"I'm proud of you already, honey. You a good daughter. I just wish Bernita was as mature and responsible as you."

"Don't worry." Maggie said. "She'll grow up one day."

With a chuckle her father said, "Lordy, I hope so for her sake."

"She will." She gave her father another big hug then watched him saunter back to the entrance of the barn. An overwhelming love for him consumed her. She thought of how hard he worked to provide for the family. He taught her how to be ambitious and to work hard to get what you wanted out of life. Maggie vowed that she would take full advantage of the opportunity given to her to help her family have a better life.

Her thoughts turned first to Bernita and then to Clarence. Once Bernita found out she was going to Philadelphia, there was no telling how difficult she would be to live with. And Clarence… she hated to leave him, but she hoped he understood why she had to go north.

***

A week later, Maggie sat in a chair in the bedroom combing and plaiting Lulu's thick mass of hair. Lulu sat on the floor at her feet, flinching and squirming.

"Be still. How can I do your hair if you keep wiggling?"

Lulu became rigid; the comb hit another snag causing her to lurch forward. "Ouch, Maggie. That hurts."

"I'm sorry. I'll try to go easier."

"So... when do the lucky one pack up for Philadelphia?" Bernita asked nonchalantly. She laid sprawled across the bed, staring up at the ceiling.

"Next month... around the first or second week of October. That way I'll be around to help with the corn and squash harvest."

"Oh, ain't you so sweet," Bernita said sarcastically.

There were more important things on her mind to let Bernita jabs get to her. As she had predicted, Bernita didn't take the news well about her going to Philadelphia. When her whining didn't have an effect, she went around the house sulking, not speaking to anyone for a few days.

"Well, it's the least I can do," Maggie replied.

"I don't want you to go," Lulu said sorrowfully.

Maggie leaned forward and hugged her around her shoulders. "I'll be back honey, in no time."

Lulu looked up at her. "How long you gonna be gone?"

"Oh, maybe a year."

Bernita gave a loud snort and turned to face Maggie, "You might be back sooner than you think."

Although she assumed Bernita was just being her usual self, she never-the-less gave her a puzzled look and asked. "Why you say that?"

"You won't last up there. You're too soft and fragile. A easy target for those slick city folks."

Indignant at her sister's taunting, Maggie frowned and gave her a harsh look, "I can just as well as anyone else."

"She jealous of you, Maggie, because she can't go," Lulu said.

"Yeah. I think so too."

Bernita bounced upright. "I ain't jealous no such a thing. I'm glad you leaving. I won't have to share the bed with 'pee the bed' Lulu anymore," she said with a smirk towards Lulu. "I can get Maggie's bed."

Lulu cast her eyes down and stuck her lower lip out. "I don't pee the bed. I only did it one time."

"Don't mind her none," Maggie said gently. "She used to pee the bed herself and it was more than one time."

Lulu covered her mouth, giggling.

Bernita rolled her eyes and flipped over on the bed, turning her back to them.

Even though the idea of going north was exciting, Bernita's words couldn't help but stir some apprehension. Afterall, she was going far away from home and everything that she knew.

Her cousin, who lived in New York, told her tales about loose women having sex with men for money. She told her about all kinds of indecent things that went on in the city; drunk men on the corners, people yelling all the time and knife fights between gangs. But that was New York. Rick never told horror stories about Philadelphia. She hoped that city proved to be different.

After Maggie finished the last plait she said, "There, Lulu. You can hop under the covers, now."

"What do Clarence think about you up and leaving him?" Bernita asked as she scooted over for Lulu to climb into bed.

"I haven't told him yet."

Her eyebrows shot up in surprise. "When you plan on telling him?"

Maggie stood in front of the mirror above the dresser and parted her hair in four sections with the comb. She grabbed a handful of the hair in the front and began braiding it.

"Tomorrow," she uttered in a hollow voice, trying to hide her trepidation of confronting Clarence with the news.

"You must not care very much for him."

"I care for Clarence with all my heart."

"Seems to me if you cared for him as much as you claim, you wouldn't just up and leave him like that."

Exasperated, Maggie turned to face Bernita. Her lips were pressed tight in anger. Bernita didn't have no right to pass judgment on her, she thought to herself. She didn't have a clue to how she felt about Clarence. She fought the urge to lash out at her.

"You're wrong, Bernita," she replied louder than she intended. She inhaled a deep breath to relax her tense muscles. Continuing in a calmer voice she said, "Not only do I care for him I love him... but going to Philadelphia is something I've always wanted to do. You know that. But it's not just for me. I'm doing it for y'all too. To help the family farm." She hated having to explain her decision to go to Philadelphia to Bernita of all people. "Once I talk to Clarence, he will understand." At least she hoped he did.

"Really. I find it hard to understand." Bernita stood up and peeled off her clothes down to her cotton slip. "If I had someone like Clarence, I wouldn't risk losing him."

No longer able to hold back her anger, Maggie blurted out, "I don't care what you think, Bernita! You don't have someone like him, so your opinion doesn't count! Besides, I don't plan on losing him!"

She saw the smirk on her sister's face but being too tired it never registered with her that Bernita was the one she could risk losing Clarence to. In fact, being too preoccupied with her own life, she never noticed the affection that Bernita had for him at all. To her Bernita was just childish and immature and needing to be the center of attention.

Maggie finished the last braid and climbed into bed, pulling the thick quilt up to her neck.

She tossed and turned, unable to sleep as Bernita's words replayed in her mind. Maybe she was right. The separation might prove too much for her and Clarence. She didn't want to risk losing the love of her life. But surely if he loved her just as much as she loved him, then what did she have to worry about?

She had been on the verge of telling Clarence several times when they were alone together, but it just never seemed to be the right moment. She knew it would be sad news for him. Although she didn't want to disappoint him, the torment of not telling him had become too much for her. She couldn't put it off any longer. She would have a talk with him tomorrow.

11

Clarence toiled among a group of fifty men, women, and children in a field that stretched white as far as the eye could see. From a distance it looked as if snow had fallen in late summer. Under the relenting rays of a blazing sun, a group of people with backs hunched over, deftly picked the cotton at a fast pace, trying to fill the large sacks slung over their shoulders. Once full, the bags were quicky replaced with an empty one, and the picking started over again.

Clarence's two younger brothers, his younger sister and two older sisters along with his parents were among the people scattered throughout the field. Picking cotton was all they knew. As soon as they were old enough to carry a bag, they were out in the fields with their parents, grandparents, aunts, uncles, cousins, and neighbors during the late summer months. Sometimes, depending on when the crop was planted, they might pick on into January. During off season they had to resort to odd jobs to bring in money until it was time to turn to the fields again to plant cotton along with other hardy crops such as peas, cabbage, and mustard greens.

Clarence stopped to fan himself with his straw hat. He pulled a grimy handkerchief out of the back pocket of his overalls and dabbed at the sweat trickling down his forehead into his eyes. The cool August weather at six that morning had turned into an unrelenting hot menace, five hours later.

An older man with a large, dingy, off white canvas bag swung over his back, limped toward him.

"How it going, Pa?" Clarence asked.

"This here four hundred pounds," he boasted.

He noticed how his father staggered, almost losing his balance, when he lifted the full sack from around his shoulder and laid it on the ground. "Pa, don't you think you should call it quits for the day. The sun way too hot. And it looks like you need a rest."

"That sun ain't bothering me non. Still got some more picking in me."

"You going to drop dead right here in this cotton field if you keep pushing yourself like you a doing."

"All I need is a little sip of water. Don't worry about me, son. I'm all right."

Clarence raised his hand to motion for the water boy. A young boy of about six years old hurried toward them carrying a large bucket of water and a dipper. His father gulped down two dippers of the water without pausing.

"Besides," his father continued after he had his fill, "If I ever plan on buying up those fifty acres at Bull's creek, I need to save me up as much money as I can."

"I know, Pa. That's why I'm doing as much as I can to help you. You can take it easy."

"I 'appreciate that, son. I sure do," he said as he picked up an empty bag to replace the full one. "But you need to stop worrying about me. I been picking cotton since I was knee deep to a grasshopper. Bout near could do it in my sleep." He placed the bag around his shoulder.

Clarence felt helpless as he watched him amble down the rows of cotton. Trying to convince him he was overworking himself was only a waste of breath. His father, even at fifty-seven years of age, still had a lot of pride and stubbornness in him.

A lot of men, and women too, by the time they reached his father's age, suffered from broken spirits and physical deterioration from working long hours, sunup to sundown, year in and year out, with little to show for their efforts.

Too many of them ended up hollowed out shells of the once young, vibrant person they used to be. Their eyes dulled from seeing a lifetime of hardships.

But determination kept his Pa going. He wanted his family out from under the sharecropping system. He wanted to farm his own land. And Clarence couldn't blame him. Even though farming was brutal work, it was well worth it not to be at the mercy of someone else. Landowners often cheated people out of payments for their labor. Most sharecroppers cleared about a hundred to two hundred dollars a year but, were so indebted to landowners for over charged fees for seeds, tools, and mules that they didn't see much of their money. It became a no-win reality for sharecroppers.

Clarence caught up with his father and began picking cotton side-by-side with him.

"When you plan on marrying that Smith gal you been courting?" his father asked.

"Well, to tell you the truth, I want to have enough money saved up to buy us a house before I ask for her hand. Plan on getting a vehicle too."

"A wise decision, son. But if I was you, I wouldn't wait too long. When you find a good woman, you don't want her to slip away. You best to go ahead and put your claim on her."

Clarence grinned. "I'll keep that in mind"

12

"Why you want to leave now Maggie? I love you. Stay and marry me. Maggie and Clarence had slipped away to their exclusive retreat under the willow tree. It was a cloudy, chilly day in late August, and they huddled together for warmth as much as for their love for each other.

Maggie placed a hand on his shoulder. "This the only opportunity I will probably ever have. I've been a wanting to go for a long time now. It's been my dream. You know that."

"I know, but don't you love me enough to let that dream go? Work is picking up for me now. I can bring in enough to support us."

"I love you, Clarence, but I'm not going just for me. My parents are in debt with the farm and could lose it if they can't get caught up. It's been tough the last couple of years or so. I can help them out by working up north."

Clarence inhaled deeply and reached for her hand, "Well, I won't stand in your way. I know what it's like when your folks need your help. I'll miss you but I'm willing to wait for as long as it takes until you come back to me."

"She searched his face, blinking rapidly to hold back the tears brimming her eyes. "You promise, Clarence?" She asked softly.

"I promise." He wiped away an escaped tear trickling down her cheek. "I love you. Nothing will keep us apart."

It was more difficult telling Clarence than she had expected. She snuggled closer to him to rest her head on his chest. Thinking about the true love they had for each other, caused her great emotional turmoil.

Clarence stroked her hair. "Don't be sad, Maggie. We gonna be together again. I promise. Philadelphia ain't forever." Reaching into his pants pocket, he pulled out an intricate carved red wooden rose. "This is for you my lovely lady," Clarence said, as he placed it in the palm of her hand.

"Oh, how beautiful! You carved this yourself?" Maggie sniffled as she examined the rose from all angles. She was stunned at how realistic it looked.

"Yep. I was waiting for a special time to give it to you. I guess now is as good a time as any."

She ran a slender finger over a smooth petal. "Thank you," she whispered.

"When you get lonely up there in that big city it'll remind you of me, and that I'll be here waiting for you."

Looking deep into his eyes she said, "I'll be back, Clarence. You can count on it."

"And when you come back, I'm hoping you'll be ready to be my wife."

"I'll be gone for a year but when I come home, I have no doubts that I'll be more than ready to be Mrs. Westbrook."

Clarence lowered his head and kissed her tenderly on the lips.

13

Maggie and Bernita took turns helping their mother with the laundry she took in from several prominent white people in the community. It was a bright, humid, Saturday morning and today happened to be Maggie's turn to help with the ironing. The way the perspiration began to bead up on her neck, was a sure sign that by noon the heat was going to be a scorcher. Hopefully the ironing was a light load that wouldn't take all day. She hated none of her other chores as much as she hated laundry day.

The Smith household did their own laundry on Mondays. Everyone in the family had a role. Buster drew the water on Sunday and poured it into two big, black wash pots in the backyard. Early the next morning Jed started the fire under the pots. The water had to be boiling hot to wash out all the accumulated mud and dirt from the field.

The clothes were first boiled in one of the pots with homemade lye soap. Afterwards, big, heavy sticks were used to beat out the dirt and stains before the items were transported to the other large pot for rinsing. After wringing the water out of the hot and heavy wet clothes, the girls spread them across makeshift clothes lines in the backyard to dry which included any nearby bushes if they ran out of space on the line. Any clothes to be pressed was done the following day. Her mother's old-fashioned method of doing laundry had been passed down from her own mother and grandmother. It was tedious work, but not having a washing machine of their own, it was their only choice to bring in a few extra dollars.

Maggie absentmindedly folded a shirt, then placed it on top of a pile of neatly folded clothes.

"You mighty quiet," her mother said as she placed the cool iron back on the bed of coals to heat up. She glanced at Maggie. "Seems to me you a be bubbling over with joy being that you're leaving next week."

Still in her own world, Maggie buttoned the buttons on a white blouse, folded the sleeves across each other in the back, then folded the blouse in half before placing it on the pile with the rest. Picking up another shirt she repeated the process, oblivious that her mother had spoken.

"Maggie!" her mother yelled to get her full attention.

Her mother's raised voice startled her out of her reverie.

"Mam?"

"What's the matter with you? Your mind a thousand miles away."

"Nothing the matter."

"I know you like the back of my hand," she said, squinting at her. "Something bothering you alright. Seems to me you should be bubbling over with joy knowing you going to be leaving in a couple of months. You having second thoughts about going north? Because if you don't..."

"No, Ma. I still want to go."

"Then, what is it?" she asked in a perplexed voice. "It ain't got nothing to do with Clarence, do it?"

Her brows furrowed in worry. She threw the shirt she was folding aside and turned to face her mother. "Ma, I just don't know if I'm doing the right thing or not. When I told Clarence I was leaving he didn't want me to go. He had expectations that we would get married soon."

"And...?" her mother said, cocking her head to one side.

"And what?"

"Is that what you wanna do?" she asked as she picked up the iron and began smoothing wrinkles out of a shirt.

"I been looking forward so to getting out of this town... living in the city...but yet..."

"Hump," her mother grunted as she readjusted the scarf tied around her head. "I been stuck right here in Hoop County all my life. Never step one foot fifty miles out of it. My life hasn't been an easy one."

"That's just it, Ma. You and Pa had a rough life and especially now with trying to keep the farm afloat. I can finally help y'all. I tried to explain that to Clarence. He said he understood but still I wonder if I'm doing the right thing."

"I tell you this, Maggie. It your decision. Sometimes it can be tough when you got to choose between following your heart or following your dreams. Sometimes you end up paying a price whichever way you go. It's up to you to decide which price you willing to pay."

Maggie watched her mother run the iron over a pair of trousers. She thought of the hardships her mother endured living the life she had no other choice but to live. Only in her fifties, she looked at least ten years older. Her hands were rough and calloused from years of picking cotton from the time she was a little girl until a few years ago when they started farming for themselves.

But life wasn't any easier as a farmer's wife. It wasn't out of the ordinary for her mother to be out in the field alongside her father determined to make a living off the land. She wanted to make sure her mother didn't have to work so hard anymore. She deserved to enjoy the finer things in life for a change.

***

While Maggie and her mother were in the back, Bernita and Lulu were in the front feeding the chicken. Bernita threw grains to the hungry chicks while Lulu ran behind a fluffy, yellow ball with feet, determined to catch it.

Bernita stopped suddenly when she saw a lone figure in a wagon approaching in the distance. The chickens swarmed around her expectantly. As the wagon drew closer, she tossed the entire pan of grains on the ground in a heap.

"Hey, Clarence!" she called out, striding to the edge of the yard to greet him.

"Hey, Bernita," he said as he hopped down from the wagon. "Where's Maggie?"

"She out back helping Ma. You can stay out front and talk to me," she offered.

Glancing at the pile of grain on the ground Clarence laughed and said, "Bout what? The right way to feed chicken?"

Bernita looked down and laughed. Then, twirling her long plait around a finger, she said coyly, "We can talk about anything you want too." She knew Maggie was close by, but it didn't matter to her. She didn't care if she heard her or not. If she wanted to flirt with Clarence, she would even if he did ignore her and not give her the time of day. One day he will take her seriously and stop treating her like a little sister, Bernita thought to herself.

Just at that time Maggie rushed around to the front of the house.

Bernita noticed how the smile on his face broadened when he saw her.

"Hey Clarence," Maggie called out, smiling back at him. "I thought I heard your voice." Turning to Bernita she asked, "Will you finish helping Ma?"

Bernita crinkled her nose. "It ain't my turn to help with the ironing."

"Please. Me and Clarence need to talk."

Bernita stood steadfast with her hands on her hips refusing to budge.

"Bernita...!" Mrs. Smith voice rang out from the back of the house.

"Coming!" she called back.

She watched as Clarence grabbed Maggie by the hand and lead her to the swing. That's okay, Clarence, she thought to herself. We'll have plenty of time for talking later.

***

The day finally arrived for Maggie to board the train for the long trip to Philadelphia. She had mixed emotions as she gave her surroundings a silent farewell. She was going to miss the place that brought her joy; the little bedroom she shared with her sisters, the Singer sewing machine sitting in the corner where she would sit for hours, and the large dirt yard where she played with her siblings. There were several things on her list, but nothing compared to how much she was going to miss Clarence.

14

It was night by the time the train pulled into the station. Maggie stepped onto the platform feeling out of place and nervous in foreign territory. As she waded through the throng of people with her old, worn-out suitcases, searching for familiar faces and watching as fellow passengers met up with waiting loved ones, a skinny colored man, with a wide brim, black hat slouched over one eye, swaggered over to her. Flicking a thick, red tongue over his bottom lips, he scanned her over from head to toe. His shifty eyes frightened her, causing a prickly shiver to run down her spine. Instinctively, she took a step backwards putting as much distance between her and the stranger as she could.

"You lost, sweetie? Need help finding somebody?" He asked with a lewd smile that flashed a sparkling, gold tooth.

"N...no. I'm waiting for my brother," Maggie stammered.

He reminded her of a slick fox, and she knew slick foxes could sneak up on chickens, snatching them away in an instant before they had a chance to run to safety.

"Well, then, baby doll," he said while slowly letting his eyes travel down her body." "Ah.... I can help you find him. A sweet, young thang like you shouldn't be all alone in this big city."

"I'm fine," she said with forced assertiveness despite her fear. "I don't need your help!"

The man threw both his hands up in the air in surrender. "Hey, just trying to be of assistance," he said with a leer before moving on.

Maggie spun around when she heard someone calling her name. It was a relief to see a heavy-set man in his mid-twenties carrying a baby in his arms, and a slim, petite woman around the same age holding the hands of two toddlers, shouldering their way through the crowd, and rushing toward her.

"Maggie!" Rick shouted again.

Overcome with excitement, Maggie yelled out, "Rick, Daisy! I'm finally here!"

They caught up with her and exchanged hugs. "Sorry we're late. I had to work a little later than usual," Rick said, panting.

"That's alright," Maggie said as she reached to take the baby from Rick's arms. "Ya'll here now." She turned her attention to the other children and exclaimed, "Look at how big they don got. They were little bitty things the last time I saw 'em. How old are they now?"

Daisy pointed to each child starting with the one Maggie was holding. "Becky here is one, Peggy's three, and David is five. Y'all tell your Aunt Maggie hi."

The two older children greeted her in quiet, shy voices.

Rick reached down to pick up her suitcases. "How's the family?"

"Fine and healthy."

"Did you have a nice trip?" Daisy asked.

"Yeah. But it was so long. I'm glad Ma fried extra chicken to last me."

Rick and Daisy laughed. "We're glad you're here," Rick said. "Well, we best get moving."

Daisy patted her on her back. "I know you must be tired. We'll show you around tomorrow."

***

As promised Rick and Daisy took her on a tour the following day. As people went about their daily hustle and bustle on South Street, Maggie noticed how well dressed some of the colored folks were; men in suits with wide legged pants and turned up cuffs; women wearing stylish suit jackets, A-lined skirts, and expensive looking shoes. Men and women both sported hats of all sorts. What she didn't see was the familiar bib overalls. She reckoned it wasn't an attire that went well with city life.

Stores lined each side of the street with clothing, jewelry, furniture, and all kinds of nick knacks. Savory smells, unfamiliar to her, permeated the air. Food stands piled high with an assortment of fruits and vegetables took up most of the sidewalk. The loud, back and forth dickering between vendors and customers startled her, but she later learned that haggling over prices was the norm. And more often than not, the customers usually won.

Daisy brought some corn and squash at one of the stands. "This corn not nearly as good as the corn Pa grows," Rick said, pulling back the husks of an ear to inspect it.

"Pa do grow some good corn," Maggie agreed. "That is, when the pests and the weather don't destroy them."

"Farmers have it tough," Daisy said with empathy. "Farming is one of the hardest jobs there is."

Rick nodded his head in agreement. "Yep. Back breaking hard work. That's why I never wanted to be a farmer."

"You never wanted to be a farmer because you too lazy." Maggie playful teasing brought laughter from Daisy and Rick.

Of course, she knew Rick was far from lazy. He was a hard worker, but he had been around during the early years when his father started out farming his own land. He saw firsthand the labor that went into having successful crops, and the pitfalls of carving out a life as a farmer. That was one of the main reasons he came north, he didn't want to follow in his father's footsteps.

Maggie nudged her way through the mass of people. Used to being polite to strangers, she was taken aback when her 'good mornings' and 'how you dos?' only received blank stares and sometimes impolite mutterings if she got in the way.

Daisy and Rick, accustomed to the brisk pace of the city, often had to stop and wait for her to catch up with them when something interesting caught her eye. There were lots of unique and wonderful things that mesmerized her, causing her to pause and linger.

Maggie saw more cars cruising up and down South Street than she had seen in her entire life. Colored folks sitting behind the wheels of Chryslers, Plymouths and Buicks thrilled her. Only a handful of folks, colored and white, back home owned cars. She didn't like, however, the constant honking of their horns, followed at times by outbursts of cursing and angry words as people strolled back and forth across the dangerous street.

A large vehicle with big wheels pulled up and stopped in front of a group of people on the sidewalk. Maggie watched as the doors flung open and the people got on and found seats. The vehicle didn't look like the picture of the street cars she saw in books. Rick told her it was one of the city buses that had replaced some of the street cars a few years ago.

Everything was new and exciting to Maggie. As she continued her stroll down the sidewalk, her head turned from side to side and a few times behind her to make sure she didn't miss anything. "I've never seen so many people in my entire life," she said with wide-eyed wonder.

Rick put an arm around her shoulder. "Welcome to the big city, lil sis. The home of brotherly love."

"What you think about it so far?" Daisy asked.

"Amazing!" She stepped toward the edge of the sidewalk and arched her neck to scan a fifteen-story, brick, and metal building looming over them. "The buildings are so tall here," she said in astonishment.

Rick and Daisy exchanged looks and laughed.

"When I was hired at the Loews Hotel, I was scared to ride the elevators at first," Rick confessed after Maggie gave him a quizzical look. "I'm afraid of heights."

Daisy laughed. "Yeah. It took him a week to get up the nerves to take the elevator just to the fifth floor without feeling like he was going to upchuck." After the laughter died down Daisy added, "We hope you have a nice stay here."

"Thank you. I appreciate y'all so much for taking me in. I hope I don't be too much of a bother."

"Honey, you know you're welcome to stay with us." Daisy said. "We wouldn't have it any other way."

Tears brimmed the corner of her eyes as it sunk in that her dream was no longer a dream. She was up north in the big city. Maggie wandered along with Rick and Daisy, turning her head this way and that way, looking up at the buildings, looking backwards over her shoulders, trying to absorb everything at once.

They crossed over the Schuylkill River bridge and came to a section of the Delaware River where eight tattered and disheveled men clustered in the doorway of a dilapidated building. The contrast of the progressive city life and these men, with their sad, vacant eyes seemed odd to her. They seemed void of life as if it had been sucked right out of them.

"They lost their jobs, homes, and families," Rick explained. "They sit here hoping for a handout to help them through another day."

Maggie was reminded of some men she saw from her train window. They had been huddling under a make-shift tent in the woods near the train tracks. Three of them ran toward the train as it crept by. She assumed that somehow, they had hopped on for a free ride in pursuit of a better life somewhere far away. Maggie dug in her pocketbook for some loose change and passed the coins out to the men who thanked her profusely.

As they continued, they came across another man standing on the sidewalk with a basket of apples and a sign around his neck that read, 'Five cents.' Rick bought two apples, giving one each to Maggie and Daisy.

The group stopped in front of a three-story building in Center City—a large sign, Stein's Sewing Factory, hung above the entrance.

Daisy nudged Maggie and pointed to the building. "That's where you going to be working."

"It is? Wow." The dull gray, towering building didn't look very welcoming to her, but she was glad nonetheless for the job.

"My boss got you signed up to start next week," Daisy said.

"Can I go inside?"

"It's closed on Sundays."

Maggie put her face to the window, but it was too dark inside to make anything out. "Will we be working together?"

"No. We'll both be on the third floor, though. You will be in the sewing room, and I'll be in the room where they tag the clothes and send them out to the stores."

"I'm nervous," Maggie said, stepping back to look up toward the third floor.

Rick gave her a playful punch on her shoulder. "No need for you to be nervous about sewing, little sis. No one a hundred miles from here can do a better stitch than you."

His compliment relaxed her. After all, she'd been sewing since she was a young girl. She laughed. "Yeah. I guess you're right." It was too late to turn back now, anyway. She would just go in Monday morning and do what she did best.

15

In the sewing room, spools of threads unwound rapidly into large swift needles causing a resounding roar. The dull beige walls along with the dimness of the overhead lights created a bleak ambience. Sunlight filtered in through two large floor to-ceiling dusty windows, alleviating some of the gloominess. The overhead gigantic ceiling fan, however, did nothing more than scatter dust and fiber particles around the stale air.

Around seventy-five women sat behind workstations absorbed in the production of sewing dresses, skirts, shirts, and pants. Maggie sat among the group. There wasn't much talking going on, except for occasional muted whispers. On one side of the worker's machines, were a pile of material already cut out for stitching. Finished garments were stacked on the other side.

A pile of skirts that Maggie had finished since starting her shift at seven-thirty that morning, sat on her worktable.

She had been given a brief orientation by the head manager upon her arrival at the factory. That included instructions on how to operate and care for her machine, her job duties, and other rules, such as bathroom and lunch breaks before she was sent out on her own.

Mrs. Johnson, the floor supervisor, roamed by each station inspecting the women's work. With her salt and pepper hair pulled back into a severe bun and an unsmiling, pale face, she looked as if she didn't tolerate any foolishness.

Squinting through skinny glasses perched halfway down her nose, she roamed the rows picking up finished garments from workstations and turning them inside out. When she came across an item that didn't meet her standards, she ripped out the seam, then threw it back onto the unfinished work pile, a low grunt the only explanation she offered.

She stopped at Maggie's station, picked up a skirt and scrutinized it keenly. She then gave her a questioning look. "You the new girl?" she asked in a gruff unfamiliar accent.

"Yes, mam," Maggie answered in a meek voice. She thought to herself that if this sour puss lady was her immediate supervisor, then working here wasn't going to be much fun.

Mrs. Johnson picked up another finished garment of hers. Her features softened as she examined it. "Mmm... good stitching. Keep up the good work." She said before wandering off to inspect another station.

A smile spread across Maggie's face, but her quick glance around the room was met with hostile stares from several women who had overheard the supervisors' praise.

When she turned to the lady sitting next to her, she was greeted however with a broad toothy smile. The lady didn't seem to be that much older than her, maybe in her early twenties. Maggie sized her up mentally. She had a hard demeanor about her as if she came from a life that hadn't been very forgiving. The aggressive way she smacked on her chewing gum made her appear tough, but her smile gave her a softer countenance.

On lunch break the women went to the lounge to eat sandwiches they brought from home. They only had thirty minutes to eat before putting the machines back in motion.

Maggie found an empty table in the section of the lounge designated for the colored workers. She sat in a folding chair and pulled a sausage biscuit out of a greasy, brown paper bag.

Even with all the machines turned off the roaring continued to echo in her ears as she began to eat.

"Mind me sitting here?" her workstation neighbor asked as she pulled out a chair.

Maggie shook her head, 'no.'

"You must be doing extra good work," she said as she sat down.

"Why's that?" she asked surprised by the statement. She was only doing what was expected of her.

The lady unwrapped a biscuit filled with ham and took a big bite. "Because old bones never give out kind words to anyone."

"I love to sew. I've been doing it most my life."

"It shows. I hear tell you from down south."

"Yep. South Carolina."

"Hush yo mouth! I'm from Georgia. Not too far from South Carolina. My name's Yvonne."

"Mine's Maggie. How long you been in Philadelphia?" she asked, thrilled to meet another southern.

"Going on six years now."

"Six years! That's a long time. Don't you miss your family?"

"I don't have no family. None that I know of, anyways. My Ma and Pa died when I was six. My grandma raised me."

When she pass away, I came up here and never looked back."

Maggie's heart went out to her. She couldn't fathom what it would be like without her family, including snooty Bernita. "It must be hard not having any family."

"Oh, you get use to it," Yvonne said in-between bites of her biscuit.

"But don't you miss Georgia?"

"That hunk of red clay? Lord no. I love it up here."

Maggie slumped her shoulders. "But things are so different and the people ain't too friendly. I don't know if I'll ever get used to this city life."

"You been out any since you been here?"

"My brother and his wife took me to see the liberty bell and they took me to a picture show..."

"No, honey. I mean you been out to any night clubs?"

"I don't go to clubs," Maggie said as if the idea of going to a club was beneath her. In her mind, night clubs were places where drunk men hung out and all kinds of immoral activities took place.

"Clubs a good way to meet men," Yvonne said, with emphasis on men. "Might make you less lonely." Her statement was followed by a boisterous laugh.

"I don't need to meet any men," she said with raised eyebrows, "I have a man waiting for me back home."

"Okay. If you say so," Yvonne said in a tone of voice that sounded to Maggie as if she didn't believe her.

After stuffing the last of her biscuit in her mouth she said, "I'm not lying. My man is back home waiting for me."

"Look. I ain't trying to get in your business, but if I was you, I wouldn't be placing no stock in thinking a man gonna be waiting back home. I tell ya, chile, I know how they is. What they say ain't always what they do."

"Well, Clarence is not like other men," Maggie said defiantly.

Before Yvonne could say another word, she got up from the table to dump her trash and then headed to the toilet designated for the colored workers before going back to work.

There were no signs on the door that said, 'colored only' or 'white only', but it was pointed out to her during orientation which bathroom to use.

***

"See you this afternoon, Maggie," Daisy said after they entered the building together one morning.

"Bye, Daisy." Maggie said as she turned to go in the opposite direction. She paused when two colored women idling in the hallway whispered to each other when she walked past them.

"She needs to burn those country rags she calls dresses," she heard one of them say. The other lady snickered, "Poor little country bumpkin. I guess nobody told her she didn't have to wear her working in the field outfits up here."

"And she talks so country. I can't understand what she's saying half the time."

The two women continued their way to the sewing room, obviously not caring if Maggie overheard them or not. Crushed, Maggie stayed planted as she watched them walk away. Looking down at her simple, cotton dress and run over shoes, she felt ashamed for the first time in her life.

Maybe Bernita had been right. She wasn't cut out for the north. She would never fit in. She ambled down the hall, fighting the urge to turn around and run down the stairs to the front entrance.

When she entered the sewing room the two women, now joined by three others, looked her way with disdain.

Maggie had to pass their station in the front to get to her workstation mid-way in the center. The women followed her with their eyes and then burst out laughing.

Maggie bristled from their taunting but held her head up, stood taller, and kept walking, looking straight ahead, but inside she felt she had shrunken by three feet. Their behavior angered her more than hurt her. Why were they so mean? What did she do to them? She pondered.

A sudden wave of homesickness overcame her. She longed to be back in familiar territory surrounded by people she knew and loved. At least in Hoop County no one ever gave her appearance a second thought.

"What's wrong, honey? Somebody don stole your last piece of candy?" Yvonne asked when Maggie flopped down in her chair.

Maggie scowled and nodded her head in the direction of the group of women. "They poking fun at me," she said. "I guess I don't dress and talk good enough to please them." Yvonne frowned, "Hump. The nerve of 'em. They ain't nobody special." She said with contempt. "I'll be right back."

"Yvonne, where you going?" Maggie whispered in bewilderment.

Sliding out of her chair, she said, "To give those heifers a piece of my mind."

Yvonne's reaction horrified her. She didn't want to be the reason for her getting fired. Maggie tried pulling her back into her seat. "Yvonne. It's okay. Just let it go."

Yvonne shook her hand away from her arm and strutted up to the women.

"Y'all up here flapping yo lips! Well, let me tell ya something. Ain't none of y'all worth the ground Maggie walk on! My grandma used to say, an empty wagon don't do nothing but make a hell of a lot of noise! That means ya'll got empty space between yo ears and is all noise!"

The women rolled their eyes at Yvonne but none of them dared challenge her.

"Don't mess with my friend, all I got to say. Or you gonna get a piece of me."

Mrs. Johnson came out of her office to stand guard in front of the room, signaling to the women to begin their work. Yvonne dashed back to her workstation just in time before the supervisor saw her.

"Don't get yourself in trouble because of me," Maggie said in a low voice.

Yvonne whispered back, "I ain't worried about them heifers. Some just like them tried to mess with me when I first came up here, too. I let 'em know right away I wasn't the one. Don't let 'em bother you."

After that day, Maggie knew she had a true friend in Yvonne.

16

By December, Maggie had become more acclimated to the city. At work she associated mostly with Yvonne. Their common southern heritage bonded them together in unity. Some of the women still snubbed her, but she loved her job too much to be bothered. Yvonne rationalized the women's behavior toward her by saying they were just jealous because she was pretty, and they were ugly. Maggie didn't care what they thought. The promise she made to her father stayed at the forefront of her mind. She vowed to work hard and make him proud of her.

Rick and Daisy taught her how to catch the bus and the subway. She managed to get lost a few times, but she soon learned the routes, often going out by herself to shop or sightsee. There was so much for her to see and do in Philadelphia, and she had the opportunity to meet people from different parts of the world. She never realized how limited her world was.

She became acquainted with an elderly white man who owned a meat shop on Market Street. He spoke broken

English with an accent so thick she had trouble understanding him. She often had to ask him to repeat himself several times. he had come from Poland ten years ago with his wife and four children, she learned. He came to America, he told her, because the opportunities were much better. He came from a very poor family of farmers in his country back home and he wanted a better life for his children.

It occurred to Maggie that even though the immigrants from other countries looked different than her, talked funny, and came from different backgrounds, they were the same in so many ways. They both longed for the same things in life– better opportunities to be able to live the best life possible.

Maggie loved going to the park with her niece and nephew. She would spend hours sitting on the bench observing the people and feeding the pigeons breadcrumbs while the children enjoyed the swing sets and slides.

Occasionally, she would find herself becoming nostalgic when something or someone reminded her of Clarence; the unique walk of a man, a robust laugh, a young couple embracing

But when she became overwhelmed by her by her emotions, all she had to do was take her carved rose out of her pocketbook to hold and caress. Stroking the cool, smooth petals helped soothe her homesickness and reminded her that Clarence was back home waiting for her return.

Rick and his family lived in a well-kept row house in South Philadelphia. It was tiny but neat with its own private bathroom. When Daisy took her to visit a few of her friends in the lower part of North Philadelphia, it had shocked her to see the horrible living conditions: buildings in need of repair, filth and garbage littering the alleys where children played; and foul odors in the hallways. To Maggie, it was worse than the sharecroppers' shacks back home.

"They call this the slums," Daisy told her. "A lot of the poor, colored and European immigrants, live here. Sometimes families of ten bunch up together in one cramped, crumbling, tenement about as small as our apartment. And the worst part, there's one bathroom on each floor."

How horrible, Maggie thought, to share one bathroom with a bunch of strangers, but then, she guessed it beat having to empty slop jars and trekking to the outhouse in the dark.

***

Maggie stood at the sink washing dishes one evening while Daisy kneaded dough at the kitchen table. The children stayed out of their way playing games in the front room while supper was underway.

The kitchen back home was dull compared to Daisy's cheerful, bright yellow kitchen. All sorts of colorful knickknacks hung on the wall and sat on shelves above the stove. The only drawback was the gas stove. She could never get the flames just right. High flames billowed upward more than once, almost torching the knickknacks, while trying to light the top burner of the range. She much preferred her Ma's old pot-bellied wood stove over the gas range anytime.

"Look like the Sloans got guests moving in," Maggie announced as she peered out the window above the sink. Across the street two adults and four young children were hauling suitcases out of a car.

Daisy walked over to look out the window, "Oh, they are Mrs. Sloan's folks from Alabama. She told me they were coming up to stay with her for a while until they get their own place. More dirt poor, colored folks pushing into the city," she added in a foreboding tone.

"Do a lot of poor people from the south come up here?" Maggie asked.

"Yes, lord. They come up north for the same reasons we did. To better themselves. Some find a way, and some don't.

Some of 'em even end up in worse off poverty than they were before.

"Why's that?" Maggie asked curiously. Until she saw the slum areas, it had never occurred to her that people could leave everything they had in the south to come north only to end up with broken dreams.

"Most colored folks are not given the chance to get the good paying jobs, especially now with jobs being hard to come by. The good jobs goes to the white folks. And if they lucky enough to get a good job they can be laid off at a moment's notice."

"That's unfair."

"Yep. Same problems we face in the south is up here too. There's a saying, 'last hired, first fired.' Only, down south you just don't get hired."

Daisy's joke brought laughter from both women, although they both knew there was truth to the saying.

In a more serious tone Daisy said, "A lot of folks have to go on public relief to feed their families. They get cornmeal, flour, grits and five dollars a month."

"Goodness! A large family can't live off that."

"Don't I know it. But the way I see it, the grain of hope of having a better life in the north is much larger than not having any hope at all in the south."

"Amen to that!"

From the living room the children yelled out, "Daddy's home! Daddy's home!"

"Hey, honey!" Daisy called out.

Rick trudged into the kitchen, carrying Becky in his arms. He gave Daisy a peck on her cheeks, "Hey, baby." Then to Maggie said, "Hey, sis." He placed Becky on the floor with a grunt, "Boy, am I tired."

"How can you be tired from riding up and down in an elevator all day?" Maggie asked, goading him. She loved teasing Rick, but she saw the frustration on his face. He had gotten laid off a few months ago from a good paying job at a steel mill, and his new job as an elevator operator cut his income in half putting a strain on the family.

"Okay. So, it ain't strenuous," Rick admitted. "Maybe that's why I'm tired. I'm bored to death. I wish I had my old job back." He paced back and forth, "I don't want to work another day in this funny looking outfit. I'm a country boy used to doing hard labor."

Maggie and Daisy exchanged amused looks.

"Well, it's true," Rick proclaimed.

"You right honey but at least for now it's getting the bills paid," Daisy said rubbing him on his back. "Supper bout ready. Peggy, David. Y'all go wash up," she ordered as she pried them away from their father's leg.

"How's work going, Maggie?" Rick asked as they sat at the table eating their meal.

"Just fine," she responded cheerfully.

"That girl is sewing her butt off at the factory," Daisy offered.

"Good. I knew my lil sis had it in her."

"I hear she's been whipping out more production than some of the girls who's been there for years."

"Is that so?" Rick asked.

"Yeah. I've been able to send Ma and Pa fifty dollars so far."

"I bet they were glad to get it."

Maggie shot fertile glances at Rick while toying with her food, "I been thinking I should move out. There's a girl at work invited me to move in with her..."

"What?" Rick interrupted in a loud voice.

His abrupt reaction shocked her, "I don't mean right away. Maybe in a few weeks. After the holidays." She hadn't figured on him being against her moving out. As far as she was concerned, he should be glad. The apartment was cramped enough without having her there. And also she didn't know how much longer she could put up with sharing a bed with her niece and nephew. Although she adored them, she about had it with them kicking and crawling all over her while she was trying to sleep.

Besides, she wanted to be independent and on her own. Rick expected her to tell him her every move and on top of that he didn't want her to go out by herself after dark. It was bad enough being treated like a child by her parents. She refused to let her brother treat her like one.

"Nope. Might as well get it out your mind," Rick said emphatically.

Maggie pushed her plate aside, "But I'll be doing y'all a favor. It's kinda crowded here. My friend has an extra room, and…"

"You only been here two months. Why you think you're be doing us a favor? We enjoy having you. And you shouldn't be by yourself in this city!"

"But I won't be by myself."

"No!" Rick said so harshly his children looked up at him, startled. Lowering his voice he said, "Ma and Pa sent you up here expecting me look out for you."

"I'm only five years younger than you, Rick. I don't need you to look after me." His implication that she couldn't care for herself annoyed her.

"Try not to rush things too fast, honey. It's not a bother having you staying with us. And you're a big help with the kids," Daisy added.

Maggie looked at Rick in resignation. There was no way she would let him boss her around. For now, though, she would just bide her time.

***

Maggie sat on the edge of the double bed she shared with her niece and nephew later that night. Retrieving a pen and paper from the bedside table, she began writing a letter with the illumination of the streetlight outside the window so she wouldn't wake them.

She paused and glanced over at the two little ones sleeping peacefully. Happy thoughts ran through her mind. She had become attached to them, and they loved their 'Auntie Maggie'. Maybe it was selfish of her for wanting to move out. After all, she should be thankful to her brother for taking her in without asking for anything in return. Sharing a bed with two toddlers wasn't the worse thing in the world.

She stared out the window and let her thoughts reflect on Clarence. She had kept up a steady correspondence with him, writing to him every week, telling him about Philadelphia and her job and always including how much she missed and loved him. He in turn wrote back confessing his love for her, saying he couldn't wait to see her again. Smiling to herself, she began writing.

'My dear, darling, Clarence. I miss you so much. You're on my mind from the moment I wake up till the time my head hit the pillow at night. Even then you are in my dreams...'

***

A few days later, several thousand miles away, Clarence stood at his mailbox reading the letter. A smile spread across his face as his eyes slowly followed each word.

'...I miss you. You are the one and only for me. Even as I get more used to living in this big city, I still miss being home with you. I sleep with your letters under my pillow every night because they bring sunshine to my lonely days. I saw a willow tree the other day and my heart melted. It brought back so many good memories of the time we shared in our special place. Tears came to my eyes but knowing you belong to me keeps me going. I can't wait until we are together again. Forever yours.

Love, Maggie.'

When he finished the last line, he started back at the top, reading it over again.

One crisp December morning, Bernita followed the trail leading from the barn to the house with a milk pail in one hand. She treaded carefully so she wouldn't stumble and spill its contents. Once inside, she set the barely half full pail on the kitchen counter and briskly rubbed the cold out of her hands.

Her mother stood at the wood-burning stove, stirring a pot of grits. Jed and Buster sat at the table eating egg biscuits.

The heat from the wood stove gave the room a nice and cozy feeling. Bernita held her numb hands over a hot burner until she could freely move her fingers again. "That has got to be the stubbornest old cow in the world," she said as she flexed and extended her fingers. "I had a hard time getting milk from her."

"That because you so mean to Betsy," Jed said. "You got to be gentle with her like Maggie use ta be."

Bernita threw him a contemptuous look. She wanted to say out loud, 'shut up dummy' but knew her mother would scold her, so instead she said it in her head. "I wasn't mean to that old cow!" she said aloud. "Betsy was the mean one. Whenever I tried milking her, she moved, causing me to miss the bucket!

Mrs. Smith walked over to the pail to see how much milk was in it. "Never mind," she said dryly. "Come on and eat your breakfast so you can get ready for church."

Bernita pushed clothes aside in the big chifforobe in the bedroom, looking for something to wear. Lulu sat on the bed pulling a thick, white sock up to her knee while eyeing her keenly.

"I'm tired of wearing the same old dresses to church all the time," Bernita mumbled to herself as she pushed a few more clothes aside. She spotted the dress Maggie wore for the spring dance. "Humm. This will do just fine," she said, taking the dress off the hanger. The cotton material was thin and summerish but that was fine by her. She would have on her coat, anyway.

"That's Maggie's dress," Lulu protested.

"So? Smart aleck. She left it here, so she must not of wanted it."

"Maggie left her dress because she forgot to pack it. She gonna be mad at you."

"Well, what she don't know won't hurt her."

Lulu watched with narrowed eyes as Bernita slid the dress over her head and stood on the bed to get a better view from the mirror over the dresser.

Admiring herself from different angles, she thought to herself that Maggie did a good job on the dress. She wished she had a talented skill like her.

Bernita turned her back to the mirror and looked over her shoulder to get a glimpse of her hips. A snug fit being she was a few pounds heavier than Maggie, but she didn't mind showing off her figure.

***

After church services, Bernita stood under a grove of trees socializing with a group of her friends when she saw Clarence shake hands with the preacher then head toward his wagon. "Clarence, wait!" she called out, taking off in his direction.

Clarence stopped and turned around.

"Want to give me a ride home?" she asked when she caught up with him.

"I don't mind if it's alright with your parents."

"Oh, they won't mind," Bernita said, climbing into the wagon seat next to him. Truth was though, she knew her parents would be angry at her for being so forward in asking a male for a ride, even if it was Clarence, but being next to him was worth facing the consequences.

Clarence pulled on the reins of the horse and yelled, "Giddy up!" The horse proceeded to trot down the road.

"What made you come to our church today?" Bernita asked.

"Your father invited me."

"I'm glad he did," she grinned at Clarence and eyed him up and down. He looked spiffy in his black Sunday suit and spit shined shoes. Bernita pretended in her mind that he belonged only to her. Gradually, she inched her way across the seat until there was no space left between them.

"That Reverend Ware can preach," Clarence said, oblivious that she had scooted closer.

"Hump," Bernita scoffed. "Pastor so old one of these days he might keel over right there in the pulpit, especially if he keeps shouting and carrying on so."

Clarence laughed, "I hope it don't happen while I'm there."

"You better not come to our church too often then," Bernita said, laughing along with him.

After their laughter subsided, Clarence glanced over at her. "You nice today," he said in a friendly tone. "Almost look like a grown up."

She gave him a push and in mock anger, said "I am grown up! In fact, I'll be eighteen next week."

"Well, well. I'll say happy birthday to you now, then."

"Thank you." He was flirting with her, Bernita thought to herself. Could it be he was coming to his senses now that Maggie was no longer around? In a hopeful voice, she said. "You want to stay and have dinner with us?"

"Thanks, but I promised Pa I'll be home to help him mend the pig pen today."

Bernita turned her body on the seat to face him. "You're a hard worker," she said sincerely. That was one of the many things she admired about him in addition to his kindness, being a gentleman and no doubt the most handsome man she's ever met.

"I try to do my best," he replied with no hint of boasting. "There's always something to be done around the home place. You know how it is."

The conversation lapsed into silence; the only sound was the clopping of the horse's iron shoes on the road. Bernita pulled her coat higher around her neck and yanked her wide, floppy, knit hat down over her ears to ward off a windy, cold breeze. "It's been two months now since Maggie been gone," she said, breaking the silence. "I suppose you miss her, huh?" She asked the question mostly to test him. To see if he was indeed having a change of heart.

"More than words can express," Clarence said wistfully.

It wasn't the answer that she wanted to hear. She creased her forehead in a frown and in a taunting voice said, "I bet she having herself a good ole time up there. It wouldn't surprise me non if she didn't want to ever come back here."

"That your opinion, Bernita. Maggie can't wait to come home. Told me so in her letters. And when she comes back, I've be right here waiting for her."

Clarence brought the horse to a stop in front of Bernita's house. She jumped to the ground then said, "The church is having their pageant on Christmas Eve next week. I get to play the Virgin Mary. You ought to come?"

"I might just do that. Should be fun seeing you on stage," Clarence said with amusement. He set the horse in motion. "By the way," he called over his shoulder as he started down the road, "That dress looks nice on you."

Bernita beamed. Two compliments in one day. She didn't care how much Clarence claimed he loved Maggie. She knew somewhere deep in his heart he had a spark for her.

18

Daisy pulled a chair from the table, propped it against the closed door of the bedroom and stood on it cautiously. She took the garland Maggie held out to her and taped it around the door frame.

Maggie had spent the afternoon helping Daisy drag boxes of decorations from the closet. With the kids' help they decorated the scrawny tree Rick had chopped down in the woods near the edge of town. Despite having to fill in some gaps between the limbs with extra ornaments, she was pleased with the results.

"This is my favorite holiday," Maggie said with a mood of melancholy as she set up the nativity scene on a side table. "I miss not being home this time of year."

"I know, honey, it's tough being away from family during the holidays. We might not be a good substitute, but at least you have us."

"Sorry. That's not what I meant. I just wish me and Clarence was spending our first Christmas together."

Daisy picked up the empty boxes and put them back in the closet. "You really love him, don't you?"

"Yeah. I do."

"Y'all have a date planned?"

Maggie placed baby Jesus in the center of Mary and Joseph then flopped down on the couch. The day that she told Clarence she was leaving flooded her mind. There was a hint of sadness in his eyes, and she felt a twinge of guilt for being the source of his pain. "Clarence had asked me to stay and marry him. I wonder if I did the right thing Daisy. Sometimes I think I should have stayed. Maybe I was too selfish thinking only of myself and not enough about his feelings."

"There's nothing wrong with taking the time out for doing something that you want to do." She turned around to discover Peggy playing with the nativity set on the table. "Peggy, baby Jesus ain't' a toy for you to play with. Put him back." Then turning her attention back to Maggie said, "If he loves you, he'll understand. He'll wait for you."

"I'm going to ask him to move up here after we get married. I don't want to live the rest of my life in Hoop County."

"You think Clarence would want to move up here to stay?"

Maggie's disposition changed at the thought of living in Philadelphia with Clarence. A smile spread slowly across her face, "I'm sure he will. I'm going to ask him to come up for a visit. I know once he sees the city for himself, he'll fall in love with it like I did."

"It will be nice to have kin folks nearby. I can't wait to meet him."

"I can"t wait for him to meet y'all too." Maggie became giddy with excitement. The possibility of him not liking Philadelphia didn't even enter her mind. It only made sense to her that he would want to get out of the south. The north had way more to offer than the cotton fields, shanties and cow pastures not to mention the Jim Crow laws.

He could get a job working in one of the factories or working at the hotel with Rick until something better came along. They would build a happy life together.

***

Maggie walked to her workstation Monday morning and slumped in her chair with a dazed look on her face .

"Well, if you don't look like the cat that ate the canary," Yvonne said." Rumor has it old bat had you in her office the best part of the morning. What gives?"

"I might get a promotion," Maggie said in disbelief. "Mrs. Johnson said I've been doing such good work with my sewing and production that I have a good chance of moving up to a garment inspector."

"Chile, that's good news.! Colored girls in this damn sweatbox don't get offers like that every day. You get to climb a notch higher on the ladder. Merry Christmas!"

"I don't believe it, Yvonne. That means I get a raise which means I can send more money home." Maggie thought about how proud her parents would be of her and how much more they could do with the extra money.

"We gotta go out tonight and celebrate. I know this jumping little joint..."

"I can't go," Maggie said quickly as she began organizing her station to begin with her work.

"Why not?" Yvonne asked, puzzled. "It's a nice jazz club. Not one of those' hole in the wall' they have back home," she said with a laugh.

"I don't know…" Maggie let her words trail off without finishing her statement. She was reluctant but a tad curious about the night life in the city at the same time.

"Oh, come on. It'll do you good to get out."

"I... don't have anything nice to wear to a club. I can't sew me up an outfit by this evening."

"Don't worry," Yvonne said with a wave of her hand. "I'm sure I got something in my closet for you. We bout the same size. I'll get you fixed up."

***

Later that evening, she caught the bus to the seventh ward to Yvonne' Rowhouse.

"Yvonne!" Maggie exclaimed when the door opened. Her friend stood in the doorway looking stunning in an elegant, short-sleeved, red velvet dress that tapered at her tiny waist and fitted snugly at her hips. "You have turned into a whole different person!"

Yvonne had parted her short hair on one side and finger waved it with pomade. Heavy eyeliner framed her eyes, and her eyebrows were a thin black line.

"You look gorgeous!"

"Thank you. I do what I do. Follow me. I have the perfect dress picked out for you,"

She followed Yvonne to the bedroom where a sleek, green dress lay on the bed. Maggie picked the dress up and stroked the fabric. "Yvonne, I can't wear this."

"Don't be silly. Of course, you can."

"But it's too expensive," Maggie gushed as she admired the dress.

"I'll let you in on a secret. I got it on sale. At the thrift store," she added. "Believe me, it didn't cost me an arm and a leg. I just pretend that it did. Go ahead. Try it on."

Maggie slipped out of her plain cotton dress and put on the low cut, form fitting dress. It outlined her curves, flattering her figure. The hem stopped at her mid-calves and the sleeves ended at her elbow. She loved the feel of the satiny fabric on her skin.

"Chile, it looks better on you than it did on me," Yvonne said. "Now, let's get your face all dolled up and a new do."

Maggie sat down in front of the vanity and closed her eyes while Yvonne expertly dusted loose powder over her face, then lined her eyes with heavy black eyeliner and mascara. Green eyeshadow was smudged on her eyelids. After rubbing a dab of rogue on her cheeks, she painted Maggie's lips with red lipstick.

When she saw her reflection in the mirror Maggie was beyond pleased with the glamorous lady starring back at her. She had never worn much make-up except for occasional lip stick.

Yvonne pinned her thick hair up in a French bun with bobby pins and a faux diamond encrusted hair clip, clipped gold ear bobs to her ears, and clasped a jeweled studded costume necklace around her neck.

"Chile, if black women could be models in one of those fancy magazines, you would be on the front cover."

Maggie stood up to examine herself in the full-length mirror hanging on the back of the closet door to get the full effect. The little country bumpkin from Hoop County had been transformed.

"This, my dear, should complete your new look," Yvonne said after pulling a coat with fake fur around the collar and a pair of shiny black high heels from the closet. After spritzing on some St Ives cologne, they were out the door.

19

Loud music blared inside the dimly lit, smokey club. Couples sat close together at tables, nursing drinks, and bobbing their heads as the musicians on the stage entertained them. A few people, mostly men, hovered at the bar near the entrance.

It was Maggie's first time inside a night club. She sashayed in behind Yvonne following her lead. More than a few men gave them approving looks as they strutted their way to a table up front near the stage. Maggie sat down and surveyed the scene of people. A man sitting alone at a table across from them winked when she inadvertently locked eyes with him. Caught off guard, she blushed and immediately riveted her focus back to the stage.

The club, although not near as large, was much nicer than the barn turned dance hall back home. The red tablecloths along with the muted lights gave it a grown-up, sexy atmosphere. The women were dressed to the nines in their velvet, sequins, and beaded gowns, making her even more appreciative that Yvonne fixed her up and gave her some nice clothes and shoes to wear. She felt she fitted in for a change. After a few moments of listening to the band Maggie leaned in toward Yvonne and said in a voice loud enough to be heard over the melodious rhythm, "This music is different from down home."

"It's called jazz. Groovy, ain't it?"

"Yeah. They can sho dish out a tune." Scanning the six musicians on stage Maggie's eyes settled on one in particular: a tall man, maybe in his mid-twenties, sporting a trim, neat mustache, and his skin a smooth, chocolate brown. The way he wore his wavy, jet-black hair slicked down on the sides with a part in the middle gave him an intriguing, dapper look.

"I like the sound of that big horn that man is playing," she said with her eyes still on him.

"Big horn?" Yvonne asked, puzzled. She followed Maggie's gaze. "No, chile, that's a saxophone," she said with a chuckle.

"Oh, really." Maggie said as more of a statement than a question. "It sounds good."

Yvonne's face lit up. "That's Benny on the sax. I know him well," she announced as if knowing him was an honor. "He's a good friend of mine. And let me tell you, he is one classy cat. I'll introduce you to him as soon as the band take a break."

"No, Yvonne," Maggie began in protest. "It ain't necessary." She thought to herself, leave it to Yvonne to embarrass her. She could be so brazen at times.

"Why not?"

With a shrug of her shoulders she simply said, "Cause..." The thought of Clarence flashed into her mind, "You know I have a boyfriend." She said finally.

"Don't be silly," Yvonne said with a wave of her hand. "Benny is cool. I'm just going to introduce you to him."

Yvonne, true to her words, motioned for the saxophone player to come over to their table as soon as the band took their break. When Maggie tried to stop her, she brushed her off

Benny, the smooth, suave, cat that Yvonne professed him to be, sauntered over to their table.

"Hey suga. Y'all playing your butts off tonight," Yvonne said.

"That's because we're playing just for you, baby," Benny said in a deep, sexy voice.

He had the thick, rich, brogue distinctive to most of the colored people born and raised in Philadelphia, not the southern drawl she was used to hearing back home. Up close he was even more impressive. Benny leaned forward to rest his hands on the table causing Maggie to catch a whiff of his robust, fragrant cologne.

"This is my friend, Maggie. We work together,"

"Nice to meet you, Maggie," he said as he extended his hand.

"We're celebrating her job promotion," Yvonne said with genuine enthusiasm.

"Good for her!"

Maggie momentarily lowered her eyes and said meekly, "Well, it's not for sure yet." She reached out to accept his hand. "Nice to meet you."

"It'll happen, Maggie. Be positive." Yvonne said with a hint of impatience in her voice.

Benny grasped her hand and held onto it longer than necessary before letting it go. Maggie felt slightly uncomfortable with the gesture, but she tried not to make anything of it.

"Let's celebrate then!" he said. "The next round of drinks on me. What you fine ladies drinking?"

"I don't drink," Maggie professed. "I'll have another ginger ale..."

Yvonne cut her off and said, "Make it two gins and tonic. It's time for this country gal to loosen up."

Benny raised his hand to signal the bartender. "Charles, my man. Take care of my friends. Whatever they want." Locking eyes with Maggie, he said. "I got to get back to my gig. It's my pleasure meeting you."

Maggie's face felt warm from the intensity of his gaze. "Nice meeting you too." After Benny left, she turned to Yvonne with a glare. "Why you do that?"

Yvonne took a sip of her drink and asked innocently, "Do what?"

"Calling that man over to our table. And you know I don't drink. Anyway, I need to head out. I promised my brother I wouldn't stay out too late."

"You a grown woman. You don't need your brother giving you a curfew."

"Yeah, but..."

"You're not in that little dirt road of a town anymore. You up here now. You got to learn how to hang. Let your hair down and have fun, chile." Yvonne held her glass up to Maggie in a toast.

Maggie hesitated then shrugged her shoulders and held her glass up, clinking it with Yvonne's. "I guess I'll drink to that," she said, Yvonne was right. She was in the north and needed to shed her backwoods image. She took a tiny sip of her drink.

"Come on," Yvonne coaxed. "Take a bigger swallow than that."

"I'm not sure I like this," Maggie said, puckering her lips.

"The taste a grow on you. Just open your mouth and take a big gulp."

Doing as suggested, she took a big swallow and immediately twisted her face in disgust bringing a gale of laughter from Yvonne. Maggie frowned, and then burst out laughing herself. "You can keep your gin to yourself. I'm getting me another ginger ale."

"Keep sipping," Yvonne urged her. "You just gotta get used to it."

Maggie gave in to Yvonne's persistence and gingerly took sips on her drink as she sat and enjoyed the music and the scene. She found herself having more fun than she had anticipated. At least there was no nosy matriarchs with watchful eyes looking for any wrongdoings to report back to her parents. She gladly accepted offers to dance.

As soon as she finished dancing with one man, there would be another one waiting his turn. Maggie felt clumsy but did her best to imitate the fast, swinging steps she saw the other couples doing on the dance floor. After observing Yvonne's exuberant dancing, she relaxed and let go of her reserve. Following her dance partner's lead, she kept up with the fast, upbeat pace.

Benny joined Yvonne and Maggie at their table after his last number. It was closing time and the piano man took over to keep the music going as people began to exit. "Did you ladies enjoy yourselves?" he asked.

"I had a wonderful time," Maggie said between heavy breathing. She had just come off the dance floor where her skillful partner had slung her up and down in the air several times. He had tried following her back to her table, but she got rid of him by turning to him and saying, "Thank you, I enjoyed the dance. Good-by." He took the hint and left her alone.

"How about you ladies joining me and my boys at the Diamond?" Benny asked.

Yvonne answered before Maggie could object. "Sounds good to me."

"What's the Diamond?" Maggie asked.

"A bar down the street," Benny offered.

Yvonne, popping her fingers said, "It don't close early like this joint. It jams all night long."

"I can't. I got to get going. You go on Yvonne. I can catch the bus home." She tucked her purse under her arm and stood up. It was already two o'clock. Rick was not going to be happy with her.

"Just like Cinderella. Rushing off before she's turned back into rags," Benny said with a chuckle.

Maggie's eyebrows shot up. She wasn't sure what he meant by the remark and wasn't sure that she liked it. "Excuse me?"

"Never mind him," Yvonne said with a wave of her hand. She picked up her clutch bag. "We came together so we'll leave together. We'll catch you some other time, sweetie," she said to Benny.

"No doubt." He turned his attention to Maggie, "I hope we can meet again."

Maggie nodded her head yes and walked off with Yvonne.

***

Light snow had begun falling by the time they boarded the bus. There were only eight other passengers on board which was nice because they didn't have to worry about finding a seat. Maggie was mesmerized by the wintry scene that rolled by outside her window. The main streets had been nicely decorated with twinkling lights, reaching across the road from poles to poles. Magical holiday scenes lit up store windows. The lights glimmering on the soft snow as it drifted down to the road was awe inspiring. It put her in a soothing and peaceful mood.

So beautiful, she thought to herself. Hoop County didn't go all out during the holiday season. In fact, the only decorations in town were strands of gold or silver garland framing door fronts and sometimes fake snow would be sprayed on the windows.

She had fallen in love with the city. She knew in her heart it was where she belonged, and one day soon Clarence would be sitting next to her on a bus sharing such a breath-taking view.

***

Maggie unlocked the door to the dark apartment and tiptoed inside, being careful not to make too much noise. She froze in her tracks when the lights suddenly flashed on.

"Where the hell you been?" Rick demanded in a loud voice. "It's three in the morning?" He was standing in the center of the room with his arms folded across his chest. Daisy, dressed in her housecoat, stood behind him in the doorway of the bedroom.

"I told you I was going out with Yvonne," Maggie said in defense.

"You didn't say you would be out cat-tailing all night." He walked closer to her and sniffed. "Have you been drinking!" he asked in a louder voice.

"Rick, not so loud. You might wake the kids," Daisy pleaded.

In a quieter tone he said, "From now on Maggie, you're not to be out after eleven."

Livid that Rick had the audacity to give her a curfew she yelled, "Rick, that's not fair! You can't tell me what to do!"

Trying to keep his voice low, Rick said, "Ma and Pa are depending on me to watch out for you. It's not safe out there in them streets. All kinds of things go on after dark...you shouldn't be out there that late."

But Maggie was defiant. She put her hands on her hips and jutted her chin forward. "I can take care of myself, Rick. I'm not a little girl anymore. You can't tell me what to do with my life!" He had taken his role as her protector too far.

"If you're gonna stay here you have to follow my rules. That's all there is to it."

Bewildered, Maggie turned to Daisy for support, but Daisy shrugged her shoulders and mouthed the words 'I'm sorry', as if she didn't want to get involved.

Rick left her with no other choice. "Well, I guess in that case I'll just move out." She stormed around him to the bedroom.

"Maggie, wait..." Daisy called out to her, but Maggie slammed the door causing the row of garlands to fall to the floor.

"What was all that noise?" Peggy asked, raising her head from her pillow with droopy, sleepy eyes.

"I'm sorry, honey," Maggie said. She stroked her niece's hair. "I closed the door too hard. Go back to sleep now."

Maggie stood in front of the window deep in thought. She didn't mean to lose her temper with Rick, but he didn't have a right to tell her what to do and when to come and go. It wasn't her intention to move out so soon. Her plans were to stay with Rick and his family a while longer but, once those words came out of her mouth, she knew it was just as good a time as any. Yvonne had been pressuring her for the longest to move in with her. She had an extra bedroom and needed someone to help cover the rent.

She glanced at the wooded, red rose sitting on the bedside table and picked it up. Holding the rose in her hands reminded her of how much she missed Clarence. She couldn't wait for his visit. She held the rose to her chest for a few moments, then placed it on the windowsill. She made a mental note to write him a letter in the morning.

20

Plans were for Maggie to wait until after the holidays to move out. The disagreement with her brother was never brought up again. Neither her nor Rick wanted to spoil the holiday spirit for the family.

On Christmas day the kids woke everyone up before the crack of dawn excited because Santa had visited them in the night. They enjoyed playing with their toys, including the gifts from their Aunt Maggie. She crafted dolls for her nieces and a hand puppet for her nephew, all from old socks, buttons, and yarn. She exchanged gifts with Daisy and Rick. They gave her a second-hand coat they bought at the thrift store.

Maggie didn't mind though. Her coat was over fifteen years old and getting too small. She gave Daisy a skirt having sewn the simple pattern at work whenever her supervisor's back was turned. She gave Rick a new tie.

She sent a box of presents home to her family. A fancy church hat for her mother, a pocket watch she bought from a street vendor for her father, yo-yos for Jed and Buster and paper dolls for Lulu. She had a hard time deciding on a gift for Bernita, knowing how picky she could be. Daisy convinced her to buy the mock jewel bracelet they saw downtown in a five and dime store.

It was Maggie's first Christmas with snow on the ground and she enjoyed it. When snow fell back home, it never amounted to more than a few inches and would be gone by evening or the next day.

The clean, sparkling, cold white stuff covering every square inch of ground; undisturbed, yet from people, animals, or cars, sitting heavy on tree branches and piled high on stoops. It reminded her of some of the Christmas cards her mother collected over the years and stored in a box under her bed.

When she was little, she used to pull the cards out from time to time to admire the beautiful scenes depicting quaint country homes surrounded by snow, Santa sitting on top of snow-covered rooftops, and a variety of snowmen.

She remembered how she used to daydream of building gigantic snowmen and snowwomen and dressing them up with old hats and scarfs. Now, with the ten to twelve inches of snow on the ground, her childhood fantasy had come to life.

After a dinner of roast hen, mashed potatoes, gravy, and green beans, topped off with apple pie, Maggie wrapped the home-made scarf around her neck that Clarence sent her. She headed outside to build snowmen with Rick and his family while singing carols. Neighbors joined in, young and old. She had so much fun she didn't have time to let her home sickness weigh her down.

Maggie drew a big heart in the snow and wrote in the center, 'Maggie loves Clarence.' She stood back to admire her handiwork, wishing for Clarence's Christmas in Hoop County to be as good as hers in Philadelphia and that the gift she sent him brought a smile to his face.

***

Clarence sat on his bed and opened the package with elated anticipation. Even though it was Christmas Eve, he couldn't wait. He was as excited as a kid. His mouth gaped open in astonishment when he saw the gift inside the box; a gray, felt, wide-brimmed hat with a wide black band. He had never owned such a fancy hat before. Clarence figured Maggie must've paid a costly price for it and he appreciated her thoughtfulness.

Some of the men at his church wore similar hats but cheaper. He had always admired how dignified they looked with their hats cocked to the side of their heads. Now he too could look just as important. And his hat was much better quality.

After putting the hat on his head, he stood up to examine his profile from the dingy, scratched, mirror hanging on the wall. He pressed it down in the top front to add a dent, tilted it low on his forehead and turned his head from one side to the other.

He was pleased with the look. He wished he had sent Maggie a nicer gift other than the scarf his mother knitted for her. She deserved something special.

Clarence grinned at the thought of one day surprising her with a ring. A ring would be a perfect gift for his perfect lady. His future wife. Yes. He would save his money and send her an engagement ring as a late Christmas present.

It was when he started to put the hat back in the box that he saw the neatly, folded letter lying at the bottom. He sat in a chair, eager as always to read her letters. His expression changed from joy, when he read about her job promotion, to sorrow, when he got to the line saying she wanted them to live in Philadelphia after they got married.

She wanted him to come up for a visit, saying that once he saw it for himself, she was sure he couldn't help but to fall in love with the city as she has, adding that she couldn't see herself ever living in Hoop County again.

The letter went on to mention her moving out of her brother's apartment to move in with a friend from work. She signed the letter, 'Love always, Maggie.' At the bottom of the letter was the address of her friend's apartment.

His eyes clouded over as he stared at the letter in his hands. No way could he ever give up the miles of green fields and fresh air to live in a city budging over with people. Maggie promised to come back to him. Now her mind seemed to have changed.

The once exuberant mood had now darkened. He promised Bernita he would come to see her in the play, but he no longer had the desire to go. Being a man of his words however, he didn't want to disappoint her. She was like a sister to him, and he knew how much it meant to her for him to see her performance. He wouldn't let her down.

After washing from the basin on the dresser and putting on clean shirt and pants, he headed for the door and then as an afterthought he turned around to grab his hat.

***

Every year the Sunday School students rotated roles in the church play. It was Bernita's turn to play the part of the Virgin Mary. Such an important role as the mother of baby Jesus gave her the jitters. She hadn't wanted the role but her Sunday school teacher, Miss Lucille, insisted that she play Mary since she usually got parts that didn't require speaking.

During practice she had a difficult time remembering what Mary said to the angel Gabrielle. Miss Lucille threatened to give the part to someone else if she didn't get it together, which suited her just fine.

But instead of keeping her threat, the Sunday schoolteacher persisted that Bernita play the role. She told her she needed to get over her stage fright, grow up and gave her a lecture about discovering the true potential inside of herself, which she couldn't discover if she hid her light behind a rock. the motivational speech only went in one of Bernita's ears and out the other. If it wasn't for Clarence coming, Benita thought while dressing backstage in her costume, she wouldn't even go out on stage. Miss Lucille could let stuck-up Susie be Mary again for the second time in a row. She didn't care.

While the cast huddled in the pastor's study waiting to begin, Bernita cracked the door open to peek out at the crowd. Her jitters subsided when she spotted Clarence sitting in the back row. When she finally went out on stage, she played her part with vigor, not stumbling over any of her lines.

"How did I do?" Bernita asked Clarence. They were standing outside sipping on the hot coca the deaconesses served after the production.

"You did good," he replied without enthusiasm.

"I was so nervous. I ain't ever doing it again." She paused and looked at his head. "Hey… I like the hat. Where you get it?"

"Maggie," he replied dryly.

Bernita chatted on, oblivious to Clarence's somber attitude. "Oh. Well, she sent us presents, too. She just wants to brag about how good she's doing up north." Extending her right arm, she said, "She sent me this bracelet. I guess it's pretty enough…"

She stopped when she realized Clarence wasn't interested in the bracelet or anything else she had to say. "What the matter? You're not acting your usual cheerful self."

"Nothing."

Bernita tilted her head to the side and narrowed her eyes, "Yes there is," she said. "I can tell. Is it because Maggie wants to stay up there in Philadelphia?"

"How you know about that?"

"She wrote to Ma and Pa saying that was what she wanted to do. That's how."

She noticed the strained tension on Clarence's face. Her heart went out to him.

"Maggie told 'em that she didn't want to come back here to live. She said she was moving in with a friend at work because Rick's place is too crowded. I guess they don't mine non, as long as she sending money home."

"You pretty nosy ain't you?" Clarence said scowling. "You seem to know a lot about what's going on."

"Well, I can't help it if they read out loud." When Clarence didn't laugh at her joke, she became concerned. In a gentle voice, she said, "I hate to be the one to say I told you so but..."

"Shut up, Bernita!" Clarence said angrily before turning to walk away.

She reached out with her hand to stop him. There was sadness in his eyes when they met hers. "Clarence...," she began, "it's not lost on me how much you care for Maggie. At one time I was hoping it was me you cared for instead of her. But now I realize that we won't ever be nothing more than friends and I accept that."

Clarence looked surprised by Bernita's confession. He opened his mouth to say something. Bernita put a hand up to signal him not to talk.

"And I'm telling you this as a friend. Don't waste your time thinking Maggie will come back to you. She has a new life going for her up in Philadelphia. I can bet you she's not sitting around doing nothing but twiddling her thumbs either. I'm sure men are flocking around her door..."

"How can you say that? You don't know what she a doing up there."

"She's my sister. I guess I know her just as well as anybody. Maggie is ambitious. She wants to see the world. That's always been a dream of hers. Hoop County is not big enough for her anymore."

"You're wrong," Clarence said defensively. "She. She's just probably mixed up right now because it's all new to her; the city lights, the excitement, and crowds of people. When she gets tired of being up there… when it all wears off…she will come back. I can count on it."

He poured the rest of his coca on the ground and ran down the steps before Bernita could say anything else.

21

Rick claimed Yvonne's neighborhood was notorious for partying and hell raising but his dire warnings didn't deter Maggie. She was ready to venture out on her own.

When she said her good-byes to her nieces and nephew, they hugged her and cried for her not to leave. The tears abated with her promise to visit on Sundays, even baby-sit them sometimes. Near tears himself, Rick tried talking her out of leaving, but to no avail. She could be as stubborn as a mule when she needed to be. Maggie assured Rick she would be safe and that he didn't have to worry about her. Plus, they were welcome to visit her whenever they wanted.

After getting off the bus in Yvonne' neighborhood lugging two large suitcases she stopped to linger for a moment to survey her surroundings. The block was much noisier than where her brother and his family lived. A group of young kids played hopscotch on the sidewalk while a group of teens lounged around on stoops carrying on boisterous conversation. It gave her a nostalgic feeling of being back home with her loud siblings. There was no doubt in her mind that she would be happy here.

***

"My crib not as big as your brother's but I hope it suits you," Yvonne said, handing Maggie a dress to hang in the closet. She was helping her unpack her meager belongings. "I'm so glad you moved in with me. Things been rough ever since my roommate moved out."

Maggie placed a folded shirt in the dresser drawer. "It's nice. I have a room all to myself. I really feel like a grown up now. No big brother around to get in my business and boss me."

"You got that right!" Yvonne said, chuckling. "Let me tell you chile, you in for some good times now! Parties are always going on around here. Matter of fact, there's a rent party on the second-floor week after next." Yvonne picked up a card from the dresser and handed it to her.

The invitation read: *If you feeling blue, I know the place where you can shake it loose. A party by Mildred & Gail. Saturday Evening, 8 until… January 10th', 1935. The invitation promised good food and music for thirty-five cents with a ticket, and forty-five cents without a ticket.*

I'll never heard of a rent party," Maggie said.

"It's a party like any other house party only you pay to get in. Mildred is helping Gail throw it to raise money for her rent. I tell you, honey, this might be a dump, but the rent is high enough to buy a house back home in one of those nicer, colored neighborhoods."

"A party sounds like fun," Maggie said.

"Chile, you better believe it." She held up one of Maggie' dresses and scrutinized its large flora pattern. "Maggie. We need to go shopping, sweetie."

Although abrasive, Maggie knew Yvonne was right. She needed new clothes. Her plain, dresses fitted in fine in Hoop County but not up here in Philadelphia. She hadn't been able to afford to buy new outfits for herself and she didn't have a sewing machine to make anything more stylish. What money she didn't send home to her folks was put aside for bills and savings. It was time for her to splurge.

***

She hit the streets with Yvonne early the following Saturday. They roamed from department store to department store on Eighth and Market Street. Maggie's feet were getting sore from all the walking. Walking for miles on the dirt packed, country roads back home was nothing compared to the hard cement of the city sidewalks.

"Why didn't you buy that cute dress you tried on back at Flynn's? Yvonne asked as they maneuvered their way across South Street along with a mob of other shoppers. "We've been shopping all morning and you ain't bought nothing yet." Yvonne carried a couple of shopping bags in her hands. Maggie's arms were empty.

"Did you see those prices! I can't believe how much clothes costs up here. How do you afford to buy them?"

"Most of the time I put things on lay-away. I figured I'll give myself a treat today."

When they approached a second-hand thrift store Maggie stopped abruptly and said, "Oh, Let's go in here."

"For what? They don't sell clothes in there."

"I know. I want to price that sewing machine in the window."

They went inside and came back out several minutes later. Maggie clapped her hands and jumped up and down.

"That machine is so nice. I can't wait to get my hands on it. I'm so glad they can deliver it tomorrow."

"You really do like to sew, don't you?" Yvonne asked, giving Maggie a quizzical look.

Maggie laughed. "Yes, I do. You ought to try it sometime."

Yvonne shifted her bags from one hand to the other and said, "I do enough of that at the factory thank you. And that's only because I have bills to pay."

"You sure you don't mind me having it? Sewing can be very noisy."

"Heavens no, chile. I'm used to it. Where to next?"

"The fabric shop."

Maggie found several bundles of cloth she liked in a store three blocks down. She bought two yards of a light blue and pink, nubby fabric and two yards of a striped, patterned cotton. Yvonne spotted a bundle of coral crepe, and convinced Maggie it would be a cute party dress.

Although it cost more a yard, she followed Yvonne's advice and bought it anyway.

"I don't know about you, but I'm starving. Let's go to Dulaney's Bakery to get a sandwich and see what kind of sweets he got on special today," Yvonne said after they exited the fabric shop.

"I'm with you," Maggie said in agreement. "A big ole slice of apple pie is what I need right now. All this shopping got my stomach rumbling."

They rounded the street corner where five teenaged boys were lounging against the corner wall. The young boys reminded Maggie of her brother, Jed, but as the ladies walked past them the boys began spewing out lewd gestures and comments.

"Hey, foxy baby!" one of the boys called out. "Ya lookin' mighty fine. Let me walk wid ya!" Another boy grabbed his crotch and said, "Yeah. Big daddy got something for ya." The other boys laughed and edged him on.

Their rowdy behavior offended Maggie. She thought to herself that her little brother would never talk so disrespectable to ladies.

Yvonne stopped and glared at them. "You boys ain't got nothing better to do than to hold up that wall! If I had some soap, I would wash yo mouth out good with it! Do your momma know you out here talking like that with your foul mouth!"

Horrified that Yvonne dared confront the boys, Maggie tugged on her arm trying to encourage her to keep walking.

Afterall, her cousin had told her some people in the city carried switch blades on them and wouldn't hesitate to slice someone up.

An older man who looked to be in his sixties bopped around the corner. He was a colorful character dressed in a tattered brown coat over a gray suit that seemed slightly too small. The sleeves of the coat stopped at least three inches from his wrist. He had on a blue button-down shirt that could use a hot iron and a multicolored necktie. On his feet were a pair of scuffed up black and white-winged tip shoes.

Maggie had never met him before, but he seemed oddly familiar to her.

"Them boys just fresh up from the country," he said with a wave of his hand toward them. "Pay 'em no mind." He had an authoritative manner about him and spoke with a thick southern drawl. He almost seemed theatrical with his exaggerated mannerism, "A lot of 'em move up here to the city and lose they country upbringing. That why they acting like jackasses. Don't know what to do with themselves now that they don't have to go out in the fields no mo."

He demanded the boys apologize to Maggie and Yvonne, which they did solemnly before sauntering off.

"Jake! How you been?" Yvonne exclaimed. "You showed up just in time. I had a mind to take a switch to them youn'um's backsides." She turned to Maggie. "Jake here is from South Carolina, too. He helps his church look out for the colored folks coming up here from down south, especially the young boys. Helps them stay out of trouble and off the chain gangs. And helped a whole lot of people find jobs."

"It's so good to have people around willing to help others," Maggie said as she shook his extended hand. "Where about in South Carolina you from?"

"Greensware. Hows abouts yoself?"

"Hoop County." It was clear now to Maggie why it seemed she knew him, his friendly, expressive demeanor was similar to some of the men she saw around town back home. Although most of them lived in poverty, they managed to exude a sense of pride even if their outfits were second- hand.

"Why, that ain't no more than a skip and a hop from my neck of the woods. I'm always honored to meet my downhome people. How long you been up?"

"I got here in October."

"Oh, a fresh newcomer. I wish you much success young lady. It takes a little time to learn the ways of city folks."

Maggie nodded her head. "I'm finding that out."

"What trouble you ladies up to on this blessed day?"

"We fixin' to go to Dulaney's to get something to eat and satisfy our sweet tooth," Yvonne said.

"Huh." Jake replied with a snarl. "Why you wants to go to his place of business? You know how his kind treat us transplants."

"How's that Mr. Jake?" Maggie asked.

"They a bunch of high-falutin group of colored folks that think they better than the rest of us," he replied bitterly. "The old Philadelphian Negro they call themselves. They don't want to see the colored folks from the south coming up here disturbing their superior way of life. If yo parents wasn't born here, then as far as they concerned you a misfit."

"Yeah, Jake. You right." Yvonne said. "But I don't let that bother me non. They can't stop us for wanting better. Besides, Mr. Dulaney is different than the rest of 'em and he sho can bake good cakes. We best get going so I can get home and let my dogs rest," Yvonne said as she shifted the shopping bags in her hands.

As the women began to walk away Yvonne turned and called out "Mildred and Gail throwing a rent party next Saturday. You comin'?"

"I jes might," Jake said. "Never knows where I might turn up. 'Specially if there's good liquor and fine ladies," he added followed with a deep, guttural laugh.

"I'll be looking for you."

"Come to church Sunday," Jake called out "And bring yo friend with you."

"Okay. We'll be there," Yvonne called back.

People were packed together like sardines in the tiny second floor apartment. The upbeat music playing on the record player could barely be heard above the incessant chattering. Couch and chairs had either been pushed up against walls or placed in the bedrooms to open space up for dancing. Booze flowed freely and everyone was seemingly having a good time.

Silvery wisps of smoke spiraled overhead as Maggie pushed and squeezed her way through the jungle of bodies in search for Yvonne. She held her hand over her nose when a puff of tobacco inadvertently drifted her way. Masculine hands reached out to get her attention and to pull her close. The nerve of Yvonne deserting me, leaving me on my own to fight off these drunk men, she thought as she shoved a hand away and kept going.

She had spent most of the evening standing by the kitchen table, nibbling on bite-sized sandwiches. Fun had stopped for her almost as soon as she arrived, especially when a group of men and women in the kitchen lit up a short, fat, rolled cigarette that emitted a strong, pungent odor. She didn't know what they were smoking, but it didn't smell like any cigarettes she ever smelt back home.

As she watched them pass the rolled cigarette around from hand to hand, she noticed that each person took a deep breath and held it a moment before blowing the smoke slowly out their mouth or nose. A couple of people had severe coughing fits after taking too deep a puff. Some of them even began acting strange after a few rounds. There were out bursts of nonstop giggling and gorging on any snacks that were handy. When the joint was passed to her, she politely declined and bolted out of the kitchen.

Maggie finally found Yvonne in a back room sitting on a man's lap with a drink in her hand. There were also a few other people coupled up in the room. Maggie walked up and tapped her on the shoulder.

"What, honey?" Yvonne asked with mild irritation.

Feeling the need to whisper, she said, "You ready to go yet?"

Yvonne bounced up and pulled Maggie to the side, "No, I ain't ready to go." She glanced back at the man in the chair. "Can't you see I'm trying to work my magic on sweet daddy over there?"

She peeked around Yvonne's shoulder to get a good look at the handsome man. He greeted her with a nod of his head. Maggie waved at him. "Who's that?" she asked.

"Luther. Benny's cousin."

"Well, you can stay if you wanna but I'm leaving."

"Why you rushing off so soon for? The party just getting started. Ain't you havin' fun?"

"I got a terrible headache," Maggie said, as she rubbed her temple to make her white lie more convincing. No. She wasn't having fun. It was way too crowded, too much noise, and more smoke than she cared to inhale. She wanted to go home, take a shower, and crawl into bed.

"I'm sorry honey. There's aspirin in the bathroom cabinet." Yvonne said with a hint of sympathy. "I'll be home later." She headed back to Luther and fell into his lap.

Once again, Maggie pushed her way through the crowd but this time heading for the front door. She bumped into someone entering as soon as she opened the door to step out. "Excuse me, miss," a male voice said apologetically.

The smooth, sexy, voice sounded very familiar. Recognition passed over her face when she took a step backward to get a good look at him. It was Benny, the saxophone player.

He studied her face a moment then grinned. "You're Yvonne's friend, Maggie?" he said with enthusiasm.

"That's right. And you're Benny. Good to see you again." She tried to step past him, but his six feet-two inches frame blocked the door.

"You're not leaving, are you?" Benny asked in disbelief.

"Yeah. I guess I am."

Looking at her intently he said in a low voice, "You can't run away from fate, baby."

Maggie stared back at him as if he had lost his mind. It was obvious he was coming on to her. She didn't know whether to be angry or to laugh. "What do you mean?" she finally asked him.

His smile broadened as he gazed into her eyes. "Fate. You know. When something's meant to be? I have a feeling we were supposed to meet again."

"Oh, you do huh?"

"Yes. I do."

Maggie could feel the heat rushing to her face. She thought she would melt from the burning glow of his gray, smothering eyes. "Well, if it was our fate to meet again, then I guess fate did its job," she tried to walk around him, but he proved to be an unmovable presence.

With a laugh he said, "Hey. Give me a chance to help fate along a bit. Maybe we could go out sometime?"

Taken aback by his forwardness she replied in a cool tone, "I'm not available. I have a boyfriend."

"And where is this boyfriend, now?"

"Down in South Carolina."

"I see," Benny stepped closer to her and in a soft whisper said, "We don't have to tell him."

With his eyes twinkling non-stop, Maggie couldn't' be sure if he was serious or only teasing her. She instinctively took a step backwards and stood gaping at him not sure how to respond to his come on.

Benny threw his arms up in surrender. "Okay. All right," he said chuckling. "What about hanging out with me as a friend?"

With a guarded expression she said, "But I don't even know you."

"I'm a nice, likeable guy. Ask Yvonne, she'll tell you. Tell you what. I'm playing at *The Joint* tomorrow night. Why don't you come out and enjoy some jazz?"

Maggie hesitated. He seemed nice enough. She guessed there was no harm in having a male friend… and she enjoyed jazz music…but she still had some reservations.

"So. Is that a plan?"

"Well…I don't…," she began.

"I promise I don't bite. It'll be nice to see a pretty face in the audience. It'll give me inspiration to play my best."

Relenting she said, "Well, okay. I guess so." She hoped by agreeing to come to the club he would be satisfied enough to leave her alone.

He tilted his head to one side. "You ain't just saying that to get rid of me, are you? You give me your word you will be there?"

Maggie laughed, "Are you always so persistent?" His charm was captivating and despite herself she was a little intrigued by him.

"When I have to be. You wouldn't let a begging man down, would you?" he asked.

"I'll be there. I promise."

"Good. Now. Can I talk you into staying a little longer?"

"No. I'm tired. I'm ready to turn in." Maggie got around him this time if only because he stepped out of her way.

When she got to the end of the hallway, she nonchalantly turned her head to look over her shoulder. Benny was leaning up against the door frame with a pleased look on his face watching her walk away.

Feeling self-conscious she halted her steps and gave him a quizzical look.

Benny nodded his head and flashed a smile.

She returned the smile and continued toward the stairs.

23

The next day Yvonne, with her hair tied up in a scarf and cream smeared on her face, sat in an overstuffed chair, polishing her long fingernails. Maggie stood at the kitchen table cutting out a pattern for a dress.

"Did you have a good time last night?" Yvonne asked as she carefully applied pink polish to her pinky finger.

"Yeah. It was alright." She figured it wouldn't do any good to tell Yvonne she had a lousy time. "There were a lot of people there."

"That's what get the rent paid, honey. Things really started jamming after you left."

"I'm glad you had fun," Maggie said frankly. Yvonne held her finger up to check out her freshly manicured nail. "Benny was disappointed you so left early."

Maggie looked up from cutting her pattern and frowned. "Why? I told him I had a boyfriend," she said in a harsh tone. "He's just being friendly. Don't get all in a tizzy."

"Yeah, well. He's friendly that's for sure. Maybe too friendly. He insisted I come to hear him play tonight."

"I know. He told me. You gonna go ain't you?"

"Well…I…I don't think I should."

"Oh, I forgot. You got a boyfriend back home."

Maggie detected the sarcasm in Yvonne's voice, but she let it slide. "Yes, I do," she replied evenly.

"Come on. Ain't like y'all going out on a date. It a do you good to get out more."

Maggie gave Yvonne a thoughtful look then asked, "Will you come with me?"

"Nope. Got me a date all lined up tonight with Luther," Yvonne replied suggestively. "Go on. Kick up yo heels. And don't say you ain't got nothing to wear. You already made yourself three new dresses."

"And I'm working on my fourth. Do you really like the outfit I made for you?" Maggie asked.

"Chile, I told you. I love it. Your dresses are better sewn than any of them fancy ones in the department stores. You should open up your own dress shop."

Maggie shrugged her shoulders, "Who knows. Maybe one day I will."

"So... you going or not?" Yvonne asked.

"Goin where?" Maggie replied innocently although she knew what Yvonne was implying.

Yvonne picked up a pillow from the couch and threw it at her. "To the club, silly!"

Maggie laughed and ducked. Then in a serious tone pleaded, "You sure you can't come with me?"

"I'm very sure. I been waiting on my chance with Luther and he's finally mine. You told him you would go so don't go backing out now."

"I guess I did, didn't I?"

"Yep, ya sure did."

Maggie didn't feel entirely comfortable meeting up with him by herself, but she gave up on trying to talk Yvonne into going with her. She couldn't help but wonder if she was trying to hook her up with Benny. It wouldn't surprise her if she had set the whole thing up. She talked non-stop about him being such a good catch and even hinted that they would make a cute couple and have pretty babies. Well, Clarence was her love, and no man could ever replace him.

And even if she was available, she didn't think she was Benny's type. He was no doubt a lady's man. Of course, she was making a judgment about him that he was but a hip, smooth talking, stylish, jazz musician who could attract a horde of women had to be a ladies' man in her opinion.

"When the last time you heard from Clarence?" Yvonne asked out of the blue.

Maggie frowned and nervously bit her lower lip. "I got a letter from him a few days after Christmas."

Yvonne gave her a keen look. "You don't seem too happy about it. Did he give you some bad news or something?"

"He said he didn't have time to come up here for a visit and that he would never want to move up north anyway." Yvonne sucked her teeth, "Hump, what a shame," she said indifferently as if she could care less.

"He wants me to come back home and marry him," Maggie said bleakly. Going back home wasn't something she wanted to do. She mistakenly assumed Clarence would accept her idea of living in Philadelphia and now she didn't know what to make of it. She needed to convince him that moving out of the south would be best for their future.

Yvonne bolted upright almost spilling her nail polish. A look of apprehension crossed her face. "You ain't going to do it, are you?"

Maggie ran a hand over the finished pattern to smooth out the wrinkles. "I don't want to, but…"

"What about your promotion? You can't just give that up!" Yvonne added as if it was beyond question that Maggie could even consider going back home. In a conspiratorial tone she said, "Woman to woman. I think you should just forget him and move on with your life."

Stunned by her bluntness Maggie sighed in exasperation. "What me and Clarence have is true love, Yvonne. How can I just forget him? What do you know, anyhow? You probably never had a man to love you the way Clarence loves me."

Yvonne rose from the couch and stood near her at the kitchen table. "It won't work, Maggie," she said with sincerity. "He don't want to move up here and you don't want to go back to Hoop County. You gonna end up getting hurt in the long run." In a more playful tone of voice she said, "You should give Benny a chance. I can tell he likes you."

Maggie narrowed her eyes suspiciously. "Why do you keep insisting on pushing me and Benny together?"

"Because y'all two are my closest friends," Yvonne replied nonchalantly. "Not too many people I can trust in this world, and I trust you and Benny. Y'all like family and I like to see my family happy."

In a way, Yvonne reasoning sounded sensible enough to her. Friends often played matchmaker to their single friends. But she wasn't single, and she wished Yvonne would stop hinting about Benny to her. She didn't need a matchmaker.

"How did you and Benny meet?" Maggie asked as she folder the cut pattern in half and then again in fourths.

"I met him when I was sixteen. Right after I moved up here matter of fact."

"You've known him for quite a while then."

"Yep. He's my buddy." Yvonne went back to her place on the couch and scrutinized Maggie closely. "Listen, I ain't told this to anyone, so don't go running your mouth. especially to those nosy heifers at work."

"I won't tell a soul," Maggie, filled with anticipation of the coming disclosure, promised as she sat on the couch next to her.

"I lied about moving up here when my granny passed. I was twelve when she died. I didn't have no other relatives to claim me, so the next-door neighbors took me in. They claimed they were only doing what God commanded them to do. Take care of the orphans. But they were sooo mean. I got a beating every other day for the least little thing. And lord If I didn't pick enough cotton! I got my tail spanked good!"

"I'm sure God didn't tell them to do that!"

"They already had six children of their own and I just became an added burden to their life. Wasn't hardly ever enough to eat. Their children got their food first. When they finished, I got the leftovers."

"Oh, my. Yvonne…"

"I lasted two years in that hell house. Couldn't take it anymore so I up and left."

Maggie, listening intently, asked, "Where did you go?"

Yvonne shifted her position on the couch and folded her legs under her. "I moved in with this older guy across town who picked beans with us during the season."

"How much older was he?"

"He was twenty-five at the time. He was nice to me at first… until he started using me for a punching bag. So, I ran again."

Maggie's mouth gaped open in shock. "Twenty-five? You were just a child! She had no idea Yvonne's life had been so rough. She never talked much about her past. "I'm sorry you went through all that, Yvonne. Where did you run to?"

"I managed to save up enough money from picking cotton for train fare. It was against the rules, but I would sneak out at night to the fields and pick cotton on my own. I hid the bags under the house and then the next day I would pay one of the neighborhood boys to take it to the gin for me to get it weighed and collect my money." Yvonne continued. "When I had enough saved up to buy a ticket, I slipped out of the house one night with my little suitcase and caught the first train heading north.

"Ended up here in Philadelphia. Broke, hungry, and nowhere to go. I slept on the streets with some other runaways around my age that I met on the train. One night an older lady who I had been seeing around town told me she owned a big house with plenty of room. She offered me free board in exchange for cooking and keeping the kitchen clean."

Maggie, sat in awe as she listened to Yvonne's revelations. "It's a good thing she took you in."

"Yeah. It was, but it wasn't because she had a good heart. She had ideas to put me working the streets."

"What you mean? She wanted you to work in the house and do some type of work in the streets too?" Maggie said in astonishment.

Yvonne made a hissing sound through her teeth. Rolling her eyes upward, she said, "Poor, chile. You don't know nothing. She wanted me to be a hooker. Sell my booty... for money. She ran a ho house," she blurted out when Maggie still looked confused.

Maggie hands flew up to cover her mouth. Her eyes wide in disbelief, "Oh, no… Yvonne. You didn't… do that did you?" she said with her hands still partially covering her mouth. Here she was, sharing an apartment with the very type of person her cousin warned her about.

Although Yvonne could be loud and coarse at times, she seemed totally different than those women standing on street corners wearing tight, revealing clothes, swishing their hips to get men's attention.

"Hold on, now. Let me finish. You asked how I met Benny. I'm getting ready to explain it to you," Yvonne interjected. "Benny was to be my first customer. I spotted him from the corner where I stood with three older, seasoned girls. He started walking our way. When he got closer, he looked dead at me. Chile, you talking about being scared outta my mind? Let me tell you, I hadn't ever done nothing like it before, but I got up the nerves and gave him my best pick up line the girls taught me. 'Hey daddy. Ya lookin' for some good times?' Yvonne mimicked seductively.

"But you know what he did?"

Maggie braced herself. "No. What?"

"He handed me five dollars and said he could help me find a real job. He said being on the streets wasn't what I needed to do with my life. I could do better for myself."

Maggie placed a hand across her chest in relief. "A real gentleman."

"Oh, he a sweetheart alright. Benny saved my life that day. No telling where I would be today if it wasn't for him. There ain't nothing I wouldn't do for that man. He saved my life."

"Were you and Benny...did y'all become...?" Maggie stammered trying to get the question out.

"Lovers?" Yvonne finished for her. "No. Benny had someone in his life at the time. Anyways, he's like a brother to me. I tell you, if it hadn't been for him, I might still be working the streets, child. All broken down and old before my time," Yvonne said with a laugh. "He recommended me to this Jewish couple to be their live-in nanny. Benny knew the man from his jigs in a band."

I guess you can't always tell a book by its cover, Maggie thought as she mulled over Yvonne's story in her mind. What Benny did for her friend impressed her. She had pegged him wrong after all.

<h1 style="text-align:center">24</h1>

Maggie caught the bus to Girard Ave in North Philadelphia at nine that night and got off two blocks from The Joint Nightclub. Wandering the streets by herself at night, in an unfamiliar part of town, filled her with some trepidation. She tried once more to talk Yvonne into coming with her, but her pleading was to no avail.

Her remembrance of what Rick said about weirdos coming out at night weighed on her mind as she headed toward the club. She shivered and shot quick, furtive glances around her. To her surprise the surrounding area seemed calm and peaceful.

Dim lights emanated from the windows of buildings and the muted voices trailing out onto the sidewalk from behind closed doors gave her comfort. A few cars occasionally passed by but mostly the road had very little traffic. There were only a few pedestrians out and about braving the cold night as they briskly hurried to their destinations. She reasoned that most people had the good sense of mind to stay inside where they were warm and comfortable. Maggie buttoned her coat up to her neck and thought to herself, she wished she had had the sense to stay home, too.

The Joint reminded Maggie of the club where she first heard Benny play: dim with similar red cloths on the square tables. Only, it wasn't as noisy which, along with the soft, sensuous, jazz, gave it a mellow vibe.

Benny winked at her when she sat down at a table near the stage. He proceeded to blow a long, soulful note into the saxophone. She smiled at him in return, then ordered a glass of wine from the waitress.

Sipping on the sweet, fruity wine helped her to unwind. She had felt nervous sitting by herself unaccompanied, but it didn't take her long to become engrossed with his solo performance. The way he drew in air and blew it out through the sax as his fingers deftly pressed buttons, produced rich, sultry melodies that fascinated her.

The instrument sung to her, and she showed her appreciation by bobbing her head to its rhythm. Before long the jazz and the wine had her fully relaxed and feeling good. She sat back and enjoyed the night with no cares in the world.

"Hey beautiful. I'm glad you came out," Benny said after his band finished their act. Another band was setting up to play for the rest of the night.

"I'm glad I came, too." Maggie said earnestly. "Hummn…I just love that jazz music."

"We have something in common then. You gonna stay for these other cats?" he asked as he sat down and pulled his chair closer to her.

"No, I don't like staying out too late."

Benny chuckled, "I've noticed that."

"I guess I best be going," she said, rising from her chair.

Benny stood and said, "I'll walk you to the bus stop."

"That's all right. You don't have to do that."

"But I wanna. I insist."

"I can catch the bus by myself. I'm a big girl." Maggie replied coolly. She didn't need him patronizing her. She had gotten enough of that from Rick.

Her reaction caused Benny to slightly flinch. "Hold on now. That's not what I meant. It's the least I can do since you came out to hear me play. After all, it is past twelve." He gave her a quizzical look. "Is that alright with you?"

There was a look of genuine concern on his face. Her guts told her he could be trusted. "Okay. I guess."

"Good. Give me time to get my sax from the dressing room." He took a step to go in the opposite direction then stopped and gave her a serious look. "Don't run off."

Maggie couldn't help but laugh at his humor.

Benny offering to walk her to the bus stop wasn't such a bad idea after all, she thought to herself. The city wasn't as eerie with him by her side. They talked about their lives as they waited at the bus stop. She told him about Hoop

County: the farming, the laundry her mother took in, and the lifestyle of the people.

He told her about life as a musician, all the traveling he's done and the things he had seen on the road. He started playing with bands throughout the city when he was fifteen and became a regular player with the band he's now with when he turned nineteen. The band tours often in Maryland, New York, Delaware, and New Jersey in addition to playing clubs in Philadelphia. "I hope to eventually find a permanent jig in Philly," he said.

"Why? Traveling to different places sounds exciting."

"It can be very exciting, but it keeps me away from home too much and that gets lonesome after a while. Besides, I want to have a family one day and see my kids grow up. Can't do that if I'm on the road half the year."

Maggie learned from him that many of his kin: a horde of aunts, uncles, and cousins, still lived in the south. His parents moved to Philadelphia along with his two older sisters and little brother when he was four. His parents instilled in him the value of family and he looked forward to starting his own one day.

The fact that Benny wanted a regular family life impressed her. He had peeled back another layer of himself.

"You plan on settling in Philadelphia?" he asked.

"Yes. I mean at least that was my plan. My boyfriend doesn't want to live up here, though."

"There're more opportunities up North for people like us."

"I know. If only I could get that in his head'.

"He ain't buying it, I gather?"

Maggie sighed. "No. I sent him a letter and suggested he come up for a visit to see for himself what it's like. He doesn't want to."

"Too busy in the fields to come up, huh?"

"This is winter," Maggie said with a laugh. "People don't farm in the winter. Except their own little plot of collards and sweet potatoes."

"Oh. Well, I guess you can tell I've never been a farmer. You should send him another letter and try harder to convince him. Remind him that there's no Jim crow laws or lynching trees up here, at least not as much as it is down south. That should be motivation enough."

"Yeah. I will keep trying."

When the bus pulled up, Benny surprised her by getting off also. "Thank you for seeing me home," she said. "I didn't expect you to ride all the way with me."

"It was my pleasure, beautiful. I enjoyed your company." He reached out and gently caressed her cheek with the back of his hand. "If you ever dump that boyfriend back home, I want to be next in line."

The touch of his hand caused goose bumps to break out on her arms. On impulse she wrapped her arms around her body to keep from shivering. His action threw her off guard. She felt confused. She loved Clarence but she couldn't help it if the way Benny looked at her made her heart quiver.

She was like a moth around a lamp in his presence drawn in by his charm. Averting her eyes from his, she told herself she needed to watch her steps around him from now on.

"Let's stay in touch," he said.

She nodded her head 'Yes' but told herself it wouldn't be such a good idea.'

25

"I wrote Clarence two more times, and I still haven't gotten a letter back from him," Maggie complained to Yvonne one day while they were on their lunch break.

Choking back tears she said, "I don't know what to think. Why did he stop writing?"

"Maybe he's trying to tell you something, honey," Yvonne replied briskly without looking up.

"Oh, really? The best way for him to tell me something is to write to me. If he no longer wants to get married, he should just tell me out right and not play with my feelings."

Not hearing from Clarence was emotionally draining. She now wished she had never suggested they live in Philadelphia. That had to be the only reason for his sudden change. He was angry and disappointed, or, her worst fear, he was courting someone else.

"That's the way men are," Yvonne said without sympathy. "They take the easy way out."

"I have a mind to write Bernita and ask her if she's seen him around with anyone else, but I don't want to give her the satisfaction. She so jealous of me she a just rub it in my face."

"Nope. I wouldn't do that if I was you," Yvonne agreed.

Maggie thought to herself, 'Yeah. Confiding in Bernita about Clarence is not the wise thing to do. If he was seeing someone else, she would gloat over it. Maybe his letters just simply got lost in the mail. That have to be it. Maybe I will hear from him in a few days.'

After days went by with still no correspondence from Clarence, Maggie became beside herself with worry. She didn't have much of an appetite to eat and started looking frail. When she woke up in the mornings her bed covers would be wadded on the floor from tossing and turning all night.

Days were spent mopping around the apartment not having the desire to do nothing more than go to work and come back home. Once home, she spent the remainder of her time in her room.

***

Yvonne was flipping an egg in the frying pan when Maggie walked into the kitchen one morning. Her mouth flew open in surprise when she turned around and took a good look at her.

"Maggie! What on earth did you do to your hair?" "Cut it off," she said flippantly.

"I can see that. But why? You had a head full of long, good hair."

"It's still good. Don't you like my new do?" Maggie asked, smoothing her hair down with both hands." She had cut her hair into a short, cropped style up to her ears, parted on one side and waved slick with pomade.

"It's not bad but you crazy to cut it."

"I needed a change."

Yvonne pursed her lips and studied her closely. "Sit down. I'll fix you some pancakes."

"I'm not hungry."

"Chile, you still pinning over that man?"

Maggie detected a hint of annoyance in Yvonne's voice. She just don't understand, 'She didn't know what it meant to love someone as much as she loved Clarence. How was she supposed to feel when the only man she ever loved just faded out of her life?' "I don't get it, Yvonne. It's just not like Clarence…"

Yvonne cut her off before she could finish. "You want to go shopping with me. Get your mind off your woes for a while."

"Naw. Sorry. I don't feel up to it."

Yvonne took a deep breath. In a voice filled with concern, she said, "Look, honey. You got to pull yourself together. Just forget about him. He's obviously ain't stuttin' about you. There plenty of fish…"

Those words out of Yvonne's mouth were like a slap in the face. Maggie bolted to her room. Yvonne called out to her, but she didn't stop. She flopped down on the bed, buried her face in the pillow.

***

One evening, a few days later, Maggie was in her room lying on her bed when she heard a knock on the front door. She heard Yvonne call out, "Benny, man! Where you been?" Out of curiosity, she eased off the bed and put her ear to the bedroom door.

"Been busy, baby. Had to go out of town for a few weeks."

"Well, you don't know how glad I am to see you."

"Why? You never been this glad to see me before," Benny said with a laugh.

Yvonne's voice hushed to a low whisper. Maggie had a difficult time hearing the conversation, but she was sure she heard her name mentioned a couple of times. Her curiosity heightened she opened the door.

Yvonne and Benny abruptly turned in her direction.

Judging by the startled expression on their faces she knew they had been talking about her.

"Hey, Benny," Maggie said without enthusiasm."

"Is that any way to greet a friend?" he asked, walking toward her.

With a forced smile she said, "I'm sorry. It's good to see you."

Benny crossed one arm across his body and cupped his chin with the hand of the other one. Cocking his head from one side to the other while keeping his gaze on her head, he nodded and said, "I like your new do. It gives you an edge. Bold and sassy."

"Thanks," she said in a flat voice.

Yvonne winked at Benny, "I'm going to go wash my hair. Maggie will keep you company while I'm gone. Won't you, honey?" She left the room before Maggie could reply.

"Why the long face, baby?" Benny asked when they were alone.

Maggie shrugged her shoulders. "Just some personal problem I'm dealing with."

"You know what? Whenever I have a problem, I go to the movies to take my mind off it. It might only be temporary, but at least it gives me something else to do besides worrying."

When she didn't respond, Benny said, "I guess, Maggie, what I'm asking is will you take in a movie with me? We won't call it a date if that'll make you feel better," he added.

At this point she figured she had nothing to lose. As far as she knew Clarence was courting someone else anyway. Maybe Yvonne was right. She needed to move on. "Okay. I'll go with you. Give me a second to get dressed."

26

A double feature, King Kong and Frankenstein, were playing for twenty-five cents at the Royal Theater on South Street West. After buying their tickets, Benny stopped at the concession stand and bought Coca Cola for each of them and a big box of buttered popcorn to share. Maggie followed him inside the darken building where he found good seats in the front row.

Just as Benny promised the films took her mind off her worries even if they were scary. She grabbed his arm when the big, angry ape beat on his chest, opened its gigantic mouth, and bellowed. When he slipped his arm around her, she didn't object and even snuggled up closer during the next showing when Frankenstein was on the verge of killing a villager.

They left the theater four hours later holding hands. When they approached a quaint, little Italian diner, Benny offered to treat her to a meal.

Maggie was in total agreement. She couldn't resist the overwhelming, spicy, aroma wafting out into the street.

"Did big bad King Kong and monster Frankenstein frighten you?" Benny asked after they ordered their food.

"No, not one bit."

Benny raised an eyebrow. "Come on now, be honest."

Maggie, trying hard to keep a straight face said, "I wasn't scared."

"Then explain why you tried to slide under the seat."

"Okay, okay. Maybe I was just a teeny bit," she said, holding her thumb and index fingers close together for emphasis.

Benny laughed. "I knew it. But that's okay. That Frankenstein is a fierce sucker. He scared me too and I most definitely wouldn't want to meet King Kong in a back ally."

Maggie laughed along with him. After her laughter died down, she gave him a thoughtful look, "Thank you Benny. I guess I did need to get out and stop staring at my four walls feeling sorry for myself."

"I'm glad you came to keep me company." Leaning in closer he said, "You want to talk about your problems?"

Toying with the metal napkin holder on the table, she said, "No. I'll rather not spoil the good time I'm having by bringing it up."

Benny grinned. "You're right. Tonight, is a night for fun and laughter. Not for a long, pitiful face."

She pulled a napkin out of the holder, wadded it up in a ball, and threw it at him. It bounced off his shoulder and landed on the floor. Maggie burst out laughing at her mischief.

"Hey, what was that for?" Benny asked, chuckling.

"I didn't have no long, pitiful face."

"Nope," he said in a low, soothing voice, "You don't now and I'm going to make sure it stays that way."

He held her gaze until she lowered her eyes timidly and blushed. She was relieved when she saw the waiter coming with their food.

"Mmmm..." Maggie murmured as she slurped a strand of noodles into her mouth. "What this called again?"

"Spaghetti. I can't believe you've never had spaghetti and meatballs."

"Well, It's the truth. I haven't. This is sooo good." Maggie attempted to twirl another strand around her fork. "Back home we eat lots of vegetables from the garden like beans, greens, turnip, corn,… and of course cornbread but never spaghetti."

"Hey, nothing wrong with that. My grandmother piles my plate with vegetables and cornbread whenever I go back home to Memphis. According to her I'm too skinny. She like saying 'you need meat on your bones so a woman can have something to hold onto," he mimicked in a shaky voice of an old lady.

Maggie laughed and then scanned his upper torso. As far as she could tell, he wasn't skinny by no means. "Nothing wrong with the meat on your bones. You got nice working in the field muscles," she said.

Benny flexed a bicep. "Thank you. Since I can't work in the fields though I just use dumb bells whenever I get a free moment."

Maggie enjoyed Benny's company more than she had anticipated. Thanks to his witty sense of humor, she forgot about everything else that was going on in her life. She felt cozy sitting in the little booth with him eating pasta and chit chatting. Having eaten very little in the past couple of weeks she finished her meal ferociously, savoring every bite.

***

It was twelve am by the time they arrived back to the apartment. There was a note left on the table from Yvonne saying she would be coming home late and not to wait up for her.

"Looks like Yvonne has plans for tonight," Benny said, after Maggie showed him the note.

"Yeah, that girl don't waste no time. She's bold enough to go after what she wants," Maggie said with a hint of admiration. "She kinda reminds me of my sister."

He leaned against the sink and asked, "Is that so? How?"

"They are both outspoken and ain't scared of nothing. Only, Yvonne is much nicer. My sister is mean," she said as she opened the refrigerator door and took out a bottle of wine.

"Are y'all close?"

"We used to be close when we were little. Seems like when she turned twelve, she started acting jealous of me."

"Humm," Benny said with his index finger poised on his lips with a pretense of deep thoughtfulness. "A little sister rivalry between you two, perhaps?"

Maggie poured wine into two glasses. She gave one to Benny and leaned against the sink next to him. "No. At least not on my part."

"If her mouth is as big as Yvonne's I feel for you, baby," he said with a laugh.

"Believe me it's way bigger."

She stood beside him sipping on the fruity wine enjoying the moment when Benny suddenly sat his glass on the counter. He took her glass from her hand and sat it next to his. In one swift motion, he put his hand under her chin, tilted her head back and kissed her tenderly on her lips.

Caught off guard she pulled away. The imprint of his lips lingered on hers. She pulled her lower lip into her mouth subconsciously. Heat rushed to her face. She felt warm all over.

"I'm falling hard for you, Maggie," Benny said hoarsely.

He pulled her closer. "When I was away on my tour all I could think about was you. I couldn't wait to see you again. That's the real reason why I stopped by today."

"But...but..," she stammered in an attempt to protest. Things were happening way too fast. She couldn't think straight.

He slowly lowered his head and whispered in her ear. "We're meant for each other. I've been looking for you all my life."

She had slipped and forgotten to watch her steps and was now at the point of no return. When his mouth found hers again, she didn't pull away. Instead, she sought his tongue with urgency. She let down her guard and returned his kisses with abandon.

Benny tightened his arms around her in a warm embrace. Her heart raced as she found herself drifting deeper and deeper into oblivion. Her breaths came in spurts. He caressed her back. She ran her fingers through his hair. Before long they were caressing each other's bodies with abandon. He nibbled on her neck causing a soft moan to escape her lips.

She let herself enjoy the sensual feelings his touch elicited. Time seemed to stand still and spiral fast at the same time. Nothing mattered to her at that moment. The stress of the last few weeks was yesterday's memories. She was at the point of no return when out of the blue she heard the front door swing open. Realizing they were no longer alone, Maggie quickly disengaged from Benny, patted her hair in place, and smoothed out her blouse.

Yvonne called out from the front room, "Hey, y'all!"

"I thought you were going to be out late," she said, trying her best to level her breathing.

"I thought so, too," Yvonne replied grimly. She took off her coat and flung it on the couch. "Luther's ex-girlfriend was at the club. That heifer! She was all over him." Through clenched teeth she muttered, "And Luther enjoyed every minute of it! The dog." Turning to Benny she added, "Tell him I don't ever want to see his sorry behind ever again."

Benny held up both hands. "Woah, wait a minute. I don't want to get involved. I tried to warn you." He then gave Maggie a kiss on her cheek. "I'll see you soon, baby. Later, Yvonne," He called out as he headed for the door. "And go easy on my cuz, alright?"

After Benny left Yvonne turned to Maggie and gave her a sly grin, "Judging by your hair all out of place it looks like you had a better time tonight than me"

Maggie smiled. "Yeah. A wonderful time." She had to admit it was the best time she's had in a while. Benny made her feel special. Their make out session was totally unexpected but surprisingly, she didn't feel any guilt about it.

Yvonne scrunched her face in mock disgust. "I'm going to bed," she said. "Life ain't fair."

Maggie went to the kitchen to top off her glass of wine. She reclined against the refrigerator door and ran a finger across her lips as the memory of the night replayed in her mind.

Later, as she was getting ready for bed, she paused and took the red, wooden rose off the bedside table where she always kept it. She held it in her hands a moment tracing the outline of a smooth petal with her finger before putting it in the bottom drawer of the dresser under her night gowns.

27

With Clarence no longer in the forefront of her mind, Maggie and Benny began dating regularly. He introduced her to a whole new world of jazz, blues, late nights at clubs, and his circle of friends. The backwoods country girl in her gradually sloughed off as she blended in with city life. She enjoyed her dates with Benny, but she kept him at arm's length, refusing to go further than let him kiss her.

One night, in a club they frequented, a blues singer on stage belted out a sultry, gut bucket blues number of how her man had done her wrong. Maggie sat nursing a gin and tonic as the poignant music put her in a melancholic, nostalgic mood. Identifying with the singer's heartbreak, she let the song take her back to the Hoop County Fair, a place she tried hard not to revisit. Clarence had taken her there on her nineteenth birthday, which was a week before she was to leave for Philadelphia.

It was a festive atmosphere on that warm, bright October day and they were so happy even though it was to be their last time together for a while. They walked around the fairground holding hands and eating cotton candy. After several chances with tossing the ring over the bottle, Clarence had proudly presented her with a stuffed lion he won as if he had slain a dozen dragons for her honor.

Maggie let out a small sigh as the memories floated through her mind. "You'll always be my lady," he told her when they got on the Ferris Wheel and waited for it to ascend. As it rose higher and higher toward the sky, she felt as if she was floating on clouds. At the time it was a moment she never wanted to forget. Now she wished she could.

She was thinking, 'it's funny how you can head in one direction that seemed so clear and end up going down a path all fuddled and full of pitfalls,' when she heard Benny calling her name.

"What's in the future for us, Maggie?" she heard through the fog that had settled over her.

"Huh?"

"I asked you what's our future? Where do you see us headed?"

How could she answer what he was asking of her? He wanted more out of their relationship. She wasn't ready to cross that line and fully commit to him. She loved being with him and everything he had to offer, yet she couldn't bear to open her heart again so soon.

Benny put his arm around her, kissing her lightly on the lips. She sat stiff and unresponsive. He tried again. She didn't return the kiss.

"You can't keep me at arm's length, Maggie," Benny said in a low voice filled with frustration, "I care for you, baby. I know you care the same for me so why have you been trying to push me away lately."

"I just don't want to rush into anything, Benny," she said.

He took his arm from around her shoulder. There was slight irritation in his voice when he spoke. "We've been seeing each other for a while now."

"I need time…"

"Time? How long is it going to take?"

Bewildered and at a loss for words she simply said, "I don't know…." The truth was, she wasn't sure what she knew. Nothing was certain anymore.

"You're afraid of getting hurt. I understand that. But believe me, Maggie, when I tell you this. I'm in love with you. I promise to never hurt you. But we can't move forward as long as Clarence still have a piece of your heart."

"I told you. Clarence is out of my life," she said with a weak voice that left room for doubt. She shifted her eyes from his stare and fingered the diamond tennis bracelet on her wrist that he bought for her from a street vendor.

He brought his face closer to hers forcing her to look into his eyes. "Are you sure about that? Be honest with yourself."

Her brows creased into a frown. Hard as she tried, moving on proved to be difficult. Just when she felt she could finally get over Clarence, she was betrayed by her emotions and reminded of the sweet, innocent love she once shared with him.

It wasn't fair to Benny. He was the perfect man of every woman's dream He proved to be nothing like the image of the jazz musician she pegged him to be. He didn't entertain a horde of women. He only wanted her. He brought out a new version of herself that she didn't even know existed, yet something still nagged at her heart as if she had unfinished business that needed settling.

"I won't pressure you anymore," he said. "I enjoy your company and when the time is right for us to take our relationship to another level you will know."

28

Spring pushed its way through the bleak winter in Hoop County. It was planting time again and men, women, and children took to the fields to prepare the earth for new seeds.

Clarence had started coming over twice a week again to help the Smith's with the sowing of their field. Upon his arrival one misty morning in April, he accepted Mr. Smith's offer to come in the house for hot coffee and buttered biscuits with blackberry preserves. After he had his fill, he thanked Mrs. Smith and went outside to wait for Jed.

Several minutes later, Bernita came outside and saw him sitting alone on the wrought iron swing. She sat on the swing beside him. "How's life Clarence?" She asked, hoping he would open up to her. She had noticed how distant he behaved in the kitchen as if his mind was miles away. He ate his breakfast in silence and didn't engage in the light-hearted banter as usual with the family.

"It moving right along," he answered in a flat tone of voice.

Never one to hold her tongue, Bernita blurted out, "Something eating at you. Spit it out."

Clarence turned his head and looked off into the horizon, as if needing to weigh the question before answering her. Turning back to face her he said in a taut voice, "I guess you was right all along bout Maggie."

"What you mean?"

"She stopped writing me. Been a while now since I got a letter from her."

So, Maggie stopped writing him, she thought to herself. And she claimed to be so in love with him. Although it pleased her that Clarence trusted her enough to share his feelings, she was concerned, nonetheless. "Why? What happened?"

"Not sure." Clarence said, rubbing the back of his neck. "Except I had wrote her and told her there ain't no possible way I could live in Philadelphia. Maybe that's why. I guess that wasn't what she wanted to hear."

Bernita, confused by what Clarence revealed to her, scrunched up her face. "What she say when you told her no?"

"She wrote back begging and pleading for me to come up there. I wrote and told her I was saving up to buy us a house, and on top of that I wanted to help my Pa get his land cleared off. But she ignored that. Her mind seemed made up. She only talked about how much she loved the city, and I should come up there to see it for myself."

Bernita noticed how Clarence's lower lip trembled as he talked about her. How could she be so cold and selfish? It was obvious he loved her very much.

"Seems she don't care nothing about my feelings... my plans... for us...," Clarence continued in a wavering voice fringed with anger. "She just stopped writing. I wrote several times more but got no letters back from her." Snapping his fingers, he said. "Just like that... it's all over." He took a deep breath and exhaled. "I guess she too busy with her new life in the city now to fool with a country boy like me."

Bernita patted him on his back and said, "Don't let it get to you. You have so much to offer. Maggie a fool for treating you this way."

Clarence took off his straw hat and rubbed a hand over of his head. "We made a promise to each other," he said in a voice tinted with sadness.

"People grow and change," Bernita replied in a flat tone.

Clarence was silent for a moment as he studied her. "Yep. I guess you're right. It seems like you changed almost overnight."

Bernita grinned. "In a good way or a bad way?" she asked, amused.

A smiled slowly spread across his face. "Definitely good. You used to be a pesky little thing; always following me around, dead on my heels."

It relieved her to see his disposition brighten., "And now?" she asked softly.

He went quiet for a moment which seemed like eternity to Bernita as she waited expectantly for his answer.

"Now, you're not only a beautiful woman but also a good friend. Thanks for helping me unburden my heart."

The fact that Clarence called her beautiful and claimed her as a friend. delighted her. "I'm glad to be your friend, Clarence. If you ever need anyone to talk to you can always count on me."

"I'll remember that."

***

Clarence and Bernita became buddies after that day, often spending time together when she could sneak away from her parents' prying eyes. Their common love of nature bonded them together. A peaceful walk in the woods tamed the wild spirit in her. It was a balm for her soul. Clarence told her he felt more alive just being in the outdoors in the fresh air, watching the animals, and taking in the scent of the earth. That was why he loved farming so much. It made him feel connected to something greater than himself. It gave him a true sense of purpose in the world.

Despite her brothers' protests, Bernita often tagged along with them and Clarence when they went fishing or exploring in the woods. To her brothers, she was not only the evil sister but a girl just in the way even if she did usually catch more fish than them.

One day Clarence took her for a ride in his wagon. They ended up in an area of woods unfamiliar to her.

"Where we at, Clarence?" she asked in amazement when he stopped the wagon in the middle of a clearance.

Clarence grinned and gestured with an outstretched arm, "This the land my Pa bought."

"Oh, my. This gonna make a nice homeplace," Bernita said as she hopped out of the wagon to take in the surrounding scenery. Tall pines and birch trees encircled a tranquil blue green pond. To her delight a bass occasionally broke the surface of the water. It thrilled her to see a rabbit scurrying across the field and stopping within five feet of her before hopping off to disappear into the covering of the deep forest.

Clarence tittered the horse and walked up to stand beside her. "Yep. But it will take some work, though, to clear back the trees and brush."

"Jed owes you and I'm sure Pa will be glad to help. And I'll do whatever I can, you know that."

"I accept the offer. Come on," Clarence said. "I'll take you on a tour." He grabbed her by the hand and together they strolled through the tall grass. They stopped at a cow pasture where ten cows and a bull were grazing. Three of the cows walked up to the fence to stare at them with big brown eyes.

"Is this pasture on y'all property, too?"

"It's on our property, but the cows and bull belong to Mr. Mooney. They don't come with the land. Pa plans on getting his own herd."

Bernita spotted a small tree full of yellow ripe plums in the center of the pasture about twenty feet away. "Ooh. Those plums look juicy. Come on, let's pick some."

Clarence looked toward the tree and a worried look came across his face. He didn't budge.

"Come on," Bernita coaxed him. "Don't be a chicken."

"I ain't chicken," he said. "Just don't see no point in disturbing that mean looking bull, yonder. I bin chased by one before and it was no fun."

"I ain't scared of no bull," Bernita said with determination. She grabbed the post and put her foot on the first rung to climb over the fence. "You stay here if you want but I'm climbing over."

By now the bull, several feet away from the plum tree, became aware of the intruders and stood still with his eyes fixed on them.

"Wait. Hold on a minute. I'll go with you." He helped her over then leaped over the fence himself in one swift motion. Together they sprinted toward the tree.

After gathering as much of the fruit in the pockets of Clarence's overalls as they could, they ran as fast as they could back to the fence and scaled it just as the bull made a charge for them.

Bernita and Clarence fell to the ground holding their sides with laughter, while on the other side of the fence, the angry bull snorted and pawed the ground with his front hoof.

***

The following Sunday afternoon, Jed, Buster, and Lulu were in the backyard playing stickball with Clarence and his two younger brothers and sister, who he sometimes brought with him when he visited the Smith's. They were around Lulu and Buster's age.

Bernita came around the corner of the house as Clarence walked up to take his turn at the bat.

"You wanna play ball with us?" Clarence asked.

"She don't know how to play no ball!" Buster shouted out.

"I do too," Bernita shot back.

"Come on then," Clarence said. "We can sho use a little help. Ain't that right, Lulu?"

Lulu rolled her eyes upward.

Bernita ran and stood near him, glad that he asked her to join them. When he handed her the stick, she stood in an awkward position over the base, pointing it straight out to her side, feigning ignorance. Lulu and Buster snickered at her pathetic lack of skill.

Clarence walked up behind her and gently re-adjusted the makeshift bat in her hands. She turned her face toward him. When their eyes met, she felt a faint fluttering in her chest. She quickly turned her head and hoped he didn't notice how fast her heart was beating.

The younger children enjoyed her playfulness of pretending she couldn't hit the ball. But unbeknownst to them, Bernita was not only athletic, but she thrived on competition. When she finally showed them her true skills, they were amazed. They appalled and cheered her on when she hit three home runs.

She had fun hanging out with Jed, Buster, and Lulu. They usually shunned and avoided her as much as possible. And usually, she didn't care. At least she told herself she didn't. She would often spend her time alone finding ways to entertain herself. It took a simple game of stickball to reconnect with them.

It felt good to be a part of the family again, and she had Clarence to thank for it happening. She didn't realize how much she had missed her brothers and sister.

29

"Watch out for that snake!" Clarence shouted out one balmy day in June while they were picking wild strawberries.

Recoiling her hand in fright Bernita yelled, "Where!"

When Clarence laughed, she pulled off a green strawberry and threw it at him. "Don't tease me. You know I hate snakes."

"That's all the more reason to watch out for 'em."

Bernita just happened to glance up as she reached for a plump, red berry. "Those clouds are low and heavy," she said with concern.

Clarence looked up toward the sky and his face immediately clouded over with apprehension. "We better head on in," he said. "It don't look good. A bad storm is rolling in."

Bernita agreed. It seemed the sky was darkening by the second with the menacing clouds.

They briskly headed towards the trail leading to Bernita's house when a rush of wind whipped the top of the pine trees back and forth.

Their fast pace turned into a gallop, but it was too late. The clouds burst into a downpour, drenching them from head to toe. The only refuge from the outburst was the weeping willow tree a few feet ahead.

Soaking wet and shivering, they huddled together under the shelter of the willow's long branches as the rain beat a steady rhythm on the hard earth

"It's a down pour," Clarence said. "I wasn't expecting this."

Bernita sneezed, then laid the bucket of berries on the ground. She crossed her arms, trying to generate some warmth. "It's downright chilly." She then peered inside the bucket. "Oh, no! I done spilled half the strawberries. I had plans on making you a pie. Now I don't have enough."

Clarence leaned back against the trunk of the tree and pulled Bernita to him, wrapping his arms around her to offer warmth from his body. "Don't worry that, non. We can always pick more. There's still plenty growing in the field."

When she snuggled up to him, he tightened his arms instinctively around her. Pleasant heat emanated from his body. She turned sideways and let her head rest on his chest while one arm casually fell at his waist. It felt good to hold him. She wanted to stay in his arms forever.

Clarence lightly stroked her shoulder with his thumb. Although she knew it was just an innocent, absent minded gesture, she delighted in his touch nonetheless and responded by lightly tracing a pattern on his lower back with the tip of her fingers. His natural, musky scent wafting through his shirt didn't repel her. In fact, it heightened her senses like a fragrant perfume.

They stood in silence, sheltered from the drizzling rain. The heady sensation of being so near created a magnetic force impossible to resist. Bernita turned her face up to him. Clarence bent his head, as if in slow motion, toward her lips. She arched her head until their lips met in unison. A soft touch on the lips became tongues entangled together.

A wave of emotions swept through her, causing her skin to tingle as if electrified. Clarence's strong arms and soft lips electrified her whole body. And just as the sudden rain burst abruptly ended so did the kiss.

Clarence quickly separated from her. He stuck his hands in his pocket and stepped backward. The distance he put between them puzzled Bernita.

"I guess we shouldn't have done that," he said remorsefully.

Her euphoria quickly diminished with the swift change in his behavior. "Why not?" she asked perplexed. "What's wrong with kissing me, Clarence?"

"It's not that... I didn't mean... we're friends." He stammered out. "Your parents trust me with you." Looking deep into his eyes Bernita said, "I love you." Clarence rubbed his hand across the top of his head.

She stepped closer to him and reached for his hand. "I've always loved you, ever since I first saw you at the church picnic. I know you have feelings for me too, somewhere deep down in your heart. You just don't want to admit it. Well, I'm in love with you and one of these days you'll say those same words to me."

She reached up and gently placed her hands on his shoulders. "I love you," she said in a soft voice. She wrapped her hands around his neck and pulled his face to hers. She brushed his lips with hers.

Although Clarence was tentative, Bernita didn't give up. She parted her lips and searched his tongue with hers until he relented to her demand.

***

"Y'all did what!" Rosa shrieked when Bernita told her what had happened under the willow tree. They had met up downtown the next day and were heading for the ice cream parlor. Rosa placed both of her hands over her heart and said dreamily, "That's so romantic. Kissing in the rain. Is he a good kisser?"

Bernita, still in a mood of pure bliss, spread her arms out to the side and twirled around in a circle. "The best."

Rosa halted her steps and looked thoughtful for a moment. In a serious, cautionary tone, she said, "You better tread careful though. You know how much he was in love with Maggie."

"He's over her," Bernita stated firmly as she proceeded to stroll at a fast pace down the sidewalk. "He ain't heard from her in a while now."

Walking briskly to catch up, Rosa said, "But what if he hasn't gotten her out of his system?"

Bernita came to an abrupt stop. Rosa was being a killjoy. She wanted to savor her tender moment with Clarence, not be reminded about his faded love for Maggie. "Listen, Rosa, I don't care. I have Clarence now and if he doesn't love me as much as he used to love her... then I'll just work on him until he does."

"Maybe you shouldn't rush in too fast. You might just be a rebound for him."

"Well, I'm not a rebound. He's over her."

"You sure of that?"

"Yes, I am," Bernita spat out as she picked up their pace again. But in her mind, she questioned if Rosa could be right.

***

Clarence's mind had been in a state of befuddlement since that stormy day. He shouldn't have let it happen, he mused one day while taking a break from his fieldwork. They crossed a boundary that friends shouldn't cross, and he didn't know where it would lead.

He couldn't deny the close bond he'd developed with Bernita. He could be himself around her. She lifted his spirits and helped him take his mind off Maggie. She was his buddy. They had good times together. But he hadn't intended for their friendship to develop into anything more.

The kiss under the willow tree happened without warning in a moment of passion. He tried to pull back, but the yearning of her soft lips swept him away. He had to admit though, that he wanted the kiss as much as she did. Maybe his feelings for her were deeper than he realized.

But she was Maggie's sister. The woman he had once been in love with and planned on marrying. Because of that, he had to make sure things didn't get out of hand. A relationship with her just wasn't possible. He didn't mean for Bernita to fall in love with him, and more than anything, he didn't want to hurt her. He needed time to sort out his feelings. He needed to clear his mind.

In the coming days, Clarence avoided Bernita as much as he could.

***

One day, a couple of weeks later, Bernita went to the back of the barn where Clarence was helping Jed mend a wagon wheel. She pretended to be engrossed in looking for poke salad, but she was really waiting for an opportunity to be alone with him. She got her chance when Jed left to go get a needed tool from the shed.

Alone finally, she walked up to him and asked accusingly, "Are you avoiding me?"

"Nope," he answered without looking at her. He was kneeling in a squatting position hammering out a crooked spoke on a wagon wheel.

"Then why is that every time you see me coming you make a beeline in the other direction? And when we are together you act like you don't want to talk to me?" Bernita pleaded. "Do I have to pretend I'm Maggie to get your full attention?"

Clarence glanced at her and went back to his task. "No. That ain't necessary. You fine the way you is, but..."

Bernita splayed her arms out in frustration. "But what? Didn't what happen between us mean anything to you?" she spat out.

Clarence stood up slowly and faced her. "Look, Bernita. Me and you... we're friends. And that's the way it should stay. What happened under the willow was a mistake. We went too far."

"How can you deny your feelings for me?" she responded in exasperation. "I opened my heart to you. Why can't you do the same? I guess I was a fool after all," she said before turning around and stomping off in a huff.

"Bernita, I... Wait...let's talk about it." But it was too late. Bernita sprinted up the trail, ignoring Clarence's call for her to come back and talk.

She refused to speak to Clarence the following days when he came over to help her father. He tried to get her attention, but still feeling hurt and angry, she would only glare at him.

Because it was picking season, the Smith family was too occupied to notice the rift between them.

30

"Silas! Silas!" Mrs. Smith called out frantically one sweltering day while the family, along with Clarence, was working in the field.

From the sound of her voice, Bernita knew something was wrong. Her father took off running to where his wife had been picking beans. Bernita was right behind him along with Jed, Buster, Lulu, and Clarence. Her mother lay sprawled on the ground looking frail and helpless.

"Gertie! Gertie! What happened?" her father called out as he knelt on the ground beside her.

"I don't know, Silas," she said in a feeble voice. "I..I ..aint feeling good. My right leg cramping real bad. Help me get up"

"Oh, lardy mercy," Mr. Smith said in panicked. He grabbed her arm and tried to help her stand but it was useless. She couldn't bear enough weight on her legs and collapsed back to the ground.

Bernita noticed perspiration forming on her mother's brow and that her face had become ashen. She put the back of her hand to her forehead. It felt cool and clammy. On instinct, she took charge. "We got to get Ma to the house. Jed, hitch up the wagon and head over to Doctor Mayfield. Tell him something awful wrong with Ma. She need help right away."

Bernita thought to herself that it was a good thing that a doctor only lived ten minutes from them being that the hospital was forty-five minutes away. They could get her to the hospital later if they needed to but right now, she needed urgent care.

"Can I go too?" Buster asked.

"Yeah, y'all hurry. Go!"

Jed and Buster took off running toward the barn.

Bernita watched as Clarence and her father cradled their arms under her mother's back and legs and carried her the hundred feet or so to the house. 'Lord have mercy. Lord have mercy…' her father kept repeating over and over. By the time they got her into the house and in bed she had passed out.

Her skin had now become very flushed and warm to the touch.

Everyone was beside themselves with worry and fright, not knowing what to expect.

Bernita remembered when her grandmother's right arm and leg became paralyzed a few years ago. The doctor told the family she had a stroke. She died shortly after being afflicted.   Bernita prayed that her mother didn't have a stroke and end up dying. She didn't know what the family would do without her.

Doctor Mayfield was at the house fifteen minutes later. Bernita led him to her mother's bedroom. To her dismay the doctor requested that everyone leave the room. Only her father was allowed to remain while the examination took place.

Lulu and Buster stood huddled near the bedroom door, wide-eyed and solemn. Although she tried her best to be strong for them, Bernita was just as scared as they were. Lulu walked up to her with her thumb in her mouth, tears streamed down her face.

"Don't cry, Lulu?" Bernita whispered. She grabbed a handkerchief from a drawer on the singer and wiped her cheeks and nose.

"Is Ma gonna die?" Lulu asked.

She wrapped her arms around her little sister and hugged her tight. "No, baby. Ma will be just fine," she said, hoping the tremor in her voice didn't betray her own uncertainty.

Buster, with his face puckering up on the verge of crying, said, "Grandma died. Ma might die too."

"Shsss. Don't say that. Have faith that she gonna pull through this." She did her best to comfort and reassure Lulu and Buster.

When Bernita glanced over at Jed sitting quietly on his bed cradling his head in his hands, compassion welled up in her chest him. She knew he was trying hard to put on a brave front, but deep down he was just as terrified as the rest of them.

Realizing that he needed something to occupy his mind she said, "Jed, why don't you take them into the kitchen and whip up something for y'all to eat, okay? It's way past suppertime. I know y'all must be starving."

At her suggestion Jed stood up and led Lulu and Buster into the kitchen.

***

Clarence had been standing unobtrusively by the front door, observing Bernita with her younger siblings. He admired her courage in the face of turmoil. She stepped up to the plate like an adult. It was a side of her he had never seen before. He was impressed.

With the kids settled in the kitchen, Bernita leaned her shoulder against her parent's bedroom door with her back to Clarence, seemingly in her own world.

He went to her and put a hand on her shoulder. "You doing good with them," he whispered.

"Bless 'em. They're scared to death,"

"And how are you doing?"

When she turned around to face him, Clarence saw the tears brimming her eyes. He wrapped both of his arms around her and pulled her to him.

"I hope I didn't tell them wrong," she said, wiping away the tears from the corner of her eyes with her fingers. "I hope Ma do recover from what she's stricken with."

"She a strong, hardy, country woman.," he said as he stroked her hair. "Like you said have faith. Let's go sit on the porch and get some fresh air."

Clarence noticed that for the first time, since he'd known her, Bernita wasn't talking a mile a minute. She sat quietly and pensive on the steps beside him. He didn't force conversation, but instead allowed her to have her moment of solitude.

He leaned back on the steps and enjoyed the warm, gentle breeze on his skin as he listened to the bullfrogs and crickets keep up a low, soothing chant. Glittering dots sparkled in the calmness of the unending, purple- black sky, giving the night perfect serenity in contrast with the upheavals of the day.

He glanced over at Bernita, and his heart quickened as memories of that rainy day under the willow tree flooded his mind. A powerful attraction for her overcame him. As he studied her profile, the words she said to him that day resurfaced, *'I know you have feelings for me somewhere deep down inside. You just don't want to admit it.'*

Maybe she had been right, he thought. He could no longer deny his feelings for her. Was it love? He couldn't say for sure, but he knew what he felt now was more than just mere friendship. Something compelled him to place an arm around Bernita and, surprising himself as much as her, he leaned in and gave her a soft kiss on the lips.

Bernita, taken off guard by Clarence's action, searched his face questionably before returning his kiss eagerly.

31

You telling me I'm not getting the promotion? Maggie asked dumbfounded. "I don't understand. Why not?" She was called into Mrs. Johnson' office early one Monday morning and was given the news that turned her world upside down. She felt as if someone had pulled the rug out from under her. She sat on the edge of her chair, looking intently at her supervisor. She prayed that there had been a mix-up and she would get the promotion after all.

Mrs. Johnson reached for a tissue and dabbed at her forehead. "I'm so sorry."

Trying her best to control her anger and frustration, she said in a level voice, "I appreciate your being sorry, but you promised me six months ago a promotion to Garment Inspector and now you sit here telling me I can't get it. I've been sewing my butt off. My production is good and none of my work is ever returned."

"Believe me, I know you do good work, but it's totally out of my hands."

"What you trying to say," she said leaning across the desk no longer caring about keeping her composure. "That I do good work but not good enough!"

Mrs. Johnson fidgeted under her intense stare.

You don't seem so tough to me right now, Maggie thought to herself. You're nothing more than a coward unable to stand up for what's right.

"I think highly of you. I really do. You're the best worker I have..."

"That's all well and good, and I appreciate that coming from you, but you still haven't explained to me why I didn't get the promotion." Maggie had her own suspicion of why, but she wanted to hear the truth come from her supervisor's mouth.

"My superiors... people above me... well they don't think you're the right person..."

"Not the right person. Why?" she asked perplexed.

"Because you're. you're..." Mrs. Johnson stammered, trying to get the words out.

Maggie finished the sentence for her. In a voice laced with venom she asked, "Mrs. Johnson, are you trying to tell me I didn't get the job because I'm colored?"

"I'm truly sorry. It was out of my hands," she said sorrowfully.

Maggie stood up to leave. "So much for the city of brotherly love. I thought things were supposed to be different up here."

She stomped out of the room, slamming the door so hard behind her that she startled some of her co-workers, but she didn't care. When she sat down at her station, she detected smirks on a few of the women's faces.

Gossip had spread like wildfire throughout the little sewing room about her being up for a promotion and some of the women had been jealous. They didn't hide their contempt by rolling their eyes at her whenever she entered the room or making snide comments such as 'Mrs. Johnson's pet' loud enough for her to overhear. She took their spiteful attitudes in stride refusing to let them rouse her.

Going now by the amused look on some of their faces, she assumed they knew that she didn't get the promotion.

One of these days I'll show them, she thought to herself.

Yvonne looked over at Maggie and paused with her task. Her eyes widened with concern. "What's the wrong? What old bat say to you?" she asked.

"I didn't get the promotion," Maggie replied in a low, weary, voice.

Yvonne looked puzzled. "And did she give you a good reason why?"

"Oh, nothing on my part… except being colored."

Shaking her head from side-to-side Yvonne said, "Some things just never change."

Not getting the promotion because of her race deeply upset Maggie, but there was nothing she could do about it.

That was the worst part, being helpless to change the bigoted notions of people. It seemed no matter how hard a colored person worked, and most of the time that meant working twice as hard, to better themselves, some people who had it in their minds that they were more superior could control their livelihood. Life is so unfair, she thought to herself.

Maggie went through the rest of the week going to work, doing her job, and keeping up with production as she's always done since starting the job nine months ago. Only, her heart wasn't in it any longer. She longed for something more than just the daily robotic grind of a nine-to-five job.

***

When Saturday rolled around, Yvonne invited her to go with her to visit a friend. Maggie declined, saying she wanted stay in and sleep late. The emotional stress of not getting the promotion, dampened her spirits. All her hopes and dreams were in the promotion, and she was beyond exhausted.

Three hours later, the shrill ringing of the telephone woke her up out of a peaceful slumber. Sliding out of bed, her eyes still heavy with sleep, she trudged to the kitchen to answer it. "Hello," she said in a groggy voice.

"Maggie," the voice on the other end said urgently. "I just got a call from Pa. Ma fell ill."

The tone of her brother's voice snapped her fully awake. "Oh no, Rick! What happened?"

"She collapsed yesterday afternoon while they were out in the field and had to be carried to the house. Pa thinks she had a stroke."

"Oh, my God! No!"

"Hold on now," Rick said reassuringly. "Pa says the doctor gives her a good chance of recovery. He didn't want to call us last night knowing we couldn't do anything until this morning. Plus, the nearest phone is ten miles away, and he didn't want to leave Ma."

"A stroke?" Maggie asked in disbelief. "He should have called anyway."

"Listen. Pa didn't want to upset you. He knew you would've been up all-night worrying," Rick said on the other end of the phone. "I'm on my way over there. Pack up a few things and we'll catch the first train heading south."

Maggie stood transfixed in a daze a few moments after hanging up the phone. She took a few deep breaths to relax her body and clear her mind then headed for the bathroom to wash up.

After getting dressed, she pulled her old suitcase out from under the bed and began packing a few items of clothing. Halfway through, she remembered to call Benny to tell him she was going out of town. She dialed his number, praying for him to pick up the phone. They had plans for a date the next day that now needed to be canceled.

She was relieved when he answered on the third ring. Trying hard to steady her voice, she said, "Benny, I can't go out with you tomorrow night. Something has happened.

Rick called and said my Ma is ill. He's on his way over here. We're catching the train this afternoon to head home."

"I'll come with you Maggie," Benny said. "I'll call Lonnie and tell him to find a replacement for me for a few days, or weeks if need be."

"That's sweet of you, Benny, but that's not necessary."

"I want to be with you at a time like this."

"I'll be fine but thank you all the same. I need to throw a few more things together. Rick will be here shortly."

"You sure you don't want me to come with you?"

"I'm sure. You have an important gig coming up that you shouldn't miss. You can't just up and leave. I'll be ok."

"I would rather be with you baby but alright if you're sure. Call me long distance to keep me posted. I will drop everything and be there at a moment's notice if you need me"

"I know you will."

"Maggie?"

"Yes."

"I ah..Have a safe trip and I'll be here waiting for you when you get back."

"Thank you."

With the last of her items finally packed, Maggie decided that she should take a light rain jacket for the sudden popup storms the south was known to have that time of year. She knew Yvonne had three light jackets and was sure she wouldn't mind her borrowing one. She planned on leaving a note to tell her what happened to her mother and that she was catching the train with Rick to go home. She would mention she borrowed the jacket in the note.

Yvonne stored her extra jackets and sweaters in a box in the back of her closet. As Maggie started to pull the box out from behind a bunch of shoes and several boxes, six letters, bound by a large rubber band, fell to the floor at her feet. She stood staring at her name on the front of the envelopes. Clarence Westbrook stood out boldly in the top left-hand corner of each one.

Baffled, she sank to the floor and hurriedly ripped one of the envelopes open. She began reading.

'Maggie, I still miss you more every day. Do you still feel the same for me? It's now been 2 months since I got your last letter and I don't know what to think anymore. Why did you stop writing? I hope it didn't have anything to do with me not wanting to live in Philadelphia. Having just bought 10 acres, you can understand my reason can't you? To have my own land been my dream for a long time Maggie. It was to be our land. What's on your mind? I need to hear from you. Please write me Maggie. I still love you." He ended the letter saying, *'I can't wait for us to be together again. I want to hold you in my arms again under our willow tree. Love, Clarence.'* The letter was dated April 14th, 1935.

She was still sitting on the floor reading the last letter when Yvonne came home earlier than expected.

"Mag-gie..." Yvonne called out gaily as she entered the apartment.

"I'm in your room!"

Yvonne halted her steps at the threshold of the door, frozen in place.

Maggie's eyes flared with hatred. "Why did you do this Yvonne?" she hissed as she scooped the letters up in her hand, waving them in the air. "You lied. You had me believing Clarence didn't want me anymore when all this time you had his letters tucked away in your closet! Why!"

Yvonne proceeded cautiously into the room. "I… I… can explain. I just wanted to help you, honey."

Jumping up from the floor, Maggie yelled out, "What you mean, help me! Me and Clarence loved each other. And now, thanks to you sticking your nose in my business, I may have lost him for good. That was a mean and spiteful thing for you to do. I can't forgive you for doing this to me. Stay out of my life!"

"Listen to me," Yvonne said with her arms outstretched in a pleading gesture. "I saw the toll it put on you when Clarence wanted you to come home and marry him and stay in Hoop County. I knew you didn't want to go back there to live. Philadelphia is where you want to be. Look. You're my best friend. I was concerned about you. That's the God honest truth."

Maggie walked toward her, closing the distance between them by only a few inches. She crossed her arms and asked, "Are you sure it was my best interest you had in mind? I just find that so hard to believe. You only think about yourself, Yvonne!"

Yvonne lowered her eyes, "Okay. Well…, to be honest it was for me too. But in a good way. She locked eyes with Maggie and said with sincerity, "You and Benny are the closest friends I have. And I don't have many. I guess, in my own selfish way, I wanted to see you two together and with Clarence out of the picture, there was a good chance. I wanted to have you both in my life. I didn't want you to leave me and move back to South Carolina."

Maggie mouth gaped open in disbelief. She couldn't believe Yvonne would stoop to such childish behavior. "You just can't take it upon yourself to interfere in other people's lives!"

"You're right and I apologize," Yvonne remorsefully.

Although the explanation wasn't making total sense, Maggie knew Yvonne well enough by now to figure out how her mind worked. There was no doubt that Yvonne genuinely thought she was protecting her by hiding the letters. Afterall, she didn't want to go back to Hoop County to live out the rest of her life. But it was wrong, nonetheless.

Maggie took a few moments to regain her composer. She needed time to process everything. Changing the subject, she said in a solemn, weary voice, "My Ma might have had a stroke. I'm heading home with Rick. He's on his way over here now."

"Oh, my!" Yvonne exclaimed.

"Rick said the doctor feels she will recover," Maggie added.

"That's good. I will keep her in my prayers."

Maggie nodded her head and said, "Thank you. I'm not sure when I will be back."

"Did you let Mrs. Johnson know you're going home?"

"Yes. I called her and told her what was going on."

A moment of tense silence filled the room. Yvonne, with a look of apprehension on her face, broke the silence and said, "I'm sorry I kept the letters from you. That was stupid of me. I don't want to lose you as a friend. I'm begging you to forgive me?"

"That remains to be seen," Maggie replied coldly. "I just hope I can set things straight with Clarence..." she paused and narrowed her eyes, "tell me something. Did Benny know about the letters?"

Yvonne shook her head rapidly from side to side. "No. He had nothing to do with it. I swear to you he didn't."

Maggie picked up the letters and headed toward the door, then stopped and turned around. "What were you going to do with these?"

"I... I don't know. Throw them away, I guess. I know you're mad," Yvonne continued when Maggie didn't respond. "And I don't blame you not one bit. I shouldn't have interfered."

Between the call from Rick and finding Clarence's hidden letters, Maggie's nerves were on edge. She would deal with Yvonne later. "I don't want to talk about it anymore," she said and left the room.

32

Maggie sat in quiet contemplation next to Rick on the long train ride heading south. Thankfully, he was napping because she wasn't in the mood for small talk. The letters from Clarence rolled around in her mind as they sped towards the Mason Dixon line. He had said he loved her and couldn't wait to see her again. She could only hope that he still felt the same. Her last letter to him was three months ago in March.

After two months of not hearing back from him, she had given up. Maggie pondered what went through his mind when her letters stopped arriving, although he was continuing to write her. Did he think the worst of her? Did he feel hurt? Angry? Betrayed? The more she thought about Clarence frame of mind, the more anxious she became. Hopefully, once she explained to him what happened, he would understand, and they could pick up where they left off. Why did she ever doubt him in the first place?

Maggie adjusted the pillow she brought along for the trip and tried to settle into a comfortable position. A grim image ran through her mind. If Bernita found out that she and Clarence hadn't spoken in months, she would be sure to throw it up in her face as proof she didn't care about him.

As she drifted to sleep, a wee voice inside her head said, but what about Benny? Maggie tried to quiet the voice and push it below the surface, but, like an apple in a bucket of water, the question kept bobbing to the surface waiting for her reply. She knew Benny cared a lot for her and she liked him but... Clarence loved her and had wanted to get married. The voice piped up again reminding her that Benny confessed his love to her, too.

Maggie pondered how different both men were. They were like night and day in comparison. Clarence, the country boy, didn't mind the hard work in the fields and a simple way of life. While Benny, on the other hand, was a city boy who lived in the world of jazz and nightclubs. She well knew of Benny's feelings for her. In fact, before finding the letters, she had entertained the thought of taking the relationship to another level. His world intrigued her, but despite everything he had to offer, after reading the letters she knew where her heart truly belonged. She still loved Clarence.

She would have a talk with Benny and explain to him that they could be nothing more than friends. If Yvonne hadn't been so meddlesome with her nosy self, Benny wouldn't even be in her life. With her mind being too confused and muddled to think clearly anymore, Maggie closed her eyes and drifted off into a deep slumber.

***

Maggie and Rick arrived at the house in the wee hours of the morning after renting a car from the Station Master, who knew the Smith family, for the long drive home.

Mr. Smith opened the door and followed Maggie and Rick into the bedroom where Mrs. Smith dozed peacefully.

"It's good she's resting well," Rick said.

Maggie stroked her mother's hair back from her forehead and kissed her. Turning to her father she said, "Pa, you go on to bed and get you some rest, okay? I'm here now. I'll help take care of Ma."

"And I'll do just that. I been so worried it done wore me plum out."

She had barely closed her eyes before being jostled awake.

Lulu, waking up to see her big sister lying next to her in bed, shrieked "Maggie, Maggie! You back!".

She raised up and tried to rub the sleep out of her eyes before reaching over to give her little sister a big, bear hug. "Hey, little Lulu. You miss me?"

"I miss you a whole lot," Lulu said. Looking up at Maggie's head she added, "I like your new hair."

"Thank you. I wacked it all off, didn't I?"

"Yeah, but it's pretty."

Bernita woke up and stretched her arms toward the ceiling. "Well, well. The prodigal daughter has returned," she said in a dry tone of voice. "When you get in?" "Early this morning around four," Maggie said.

"Did Peggy and David come with you?" Lulu asked.

"No. Just Rick. Daisy said she'll try to come home with the kids next months. She couldn't get off from work." Maggie's head felt heavy with sleep. "What time is it?" she asked with a yawn.

"Six-thirty," Bernita said as she rolled onto her side to sit on the edge of the bed. "Come on, Lulu, we best get breakfast started so we don't end up being late for church."

After they left the room, Maggie turned over and went back to sleep.

Everyone had finished eating by the time she came down into the kitchen three hours later.

Bernita, busy putting the breakfast dishes away, shot Maggie a sideways glance. "There're grits left over and biscuits in the oven."

"Humm. Hot buttered biscuits and some of Ma's blackberry preserves sounds good."

"How long you plan on staying?" Bernita asked matter-of-factly as Maggie dipped preserves onto a plate.

"I don't know... I guess until ma is up on her feet again."

"The doctor says she should be up and about in a few days. She didn't need to go to the hospital. It was heat exhaustion not a stroke like we thought."

"Good that it wasn't a stoke but she looks weak and feeble. Poor Pa. It must be hard on him to see Ma laid up like that. I'm glad I could come home and help take care of things." Bernita whirled around. "You didn't have to come home to help take care of things. We're doing just fine."

Baffled by Bernita's outburst Maggie said, "I'm sure y'all are. Now that I'm here I can do my part to help is what I mean."

Umn," Bernita said pursing her lips. "Seems to me like you were liking it so much in Philadelphia you wanted to desert the family and stay up there."

Maggie exhaled a long, deep breath. "Bernita, I just got here. I don't want to start with you. I've been very busy working my ass off in Philadelphia. That's how I been able to send money home, or did you forget why I left in the first place? When will you stop being so jealous of me?

"I ain't no such a thing! Why should I be jealous of you? You going up north and coming back all siddity and talking proper, don't mean a hill of beans to me. I guess you think you somebody special now," Bernita said as she grabbed the milk bucket and rushed out the back door before Maggie could respond.

Maggie tried to finish her biscuits and blackberry preserves, but her conversation with Bernita left a lump in her throat. With her being away for a while she had hoped she would have changed and grew up a little. But nope. She was her same old spiteful self.

As soon as she had managed to eat the last bite of preserves and biscuit, she heard the front door open and then a deep, male voice greeting Jed. It was Clarence's voice. She would recognize it anywhere. She hadn't expected to see him so soon. Excited and anxious at the same time, her heart pounded as she opened the door leading to the living room.

"Clarence...," Maggie began cheerfully only to stop dead in her tracks when she saw the loathsome expression on his face He had been in deep conversation with Jed, but as soon as he saw her the smile on his face dissolved in a flash.

"How you doing, Maggie?" he said in a tight voice. "I stopped by to pay your Ma a visit and wish her well before I head on to church."

His cold greeting disappointed her. She wasn't sure what to expect when they'd finally meet again, but she didn't expect such a detached attitude from him. He didn't seem happy at all to see her. Could the memories of their joyous times together fade so easily from his mind despite their misunderstanding? "I'm fine," she said, fidgeting with her hair. His hostile scrutiny made her uncomfortable. "I'm sure she'll be glad you came by."

Jed looked from Maggie to Clarence, then shrugged his shoulders and said, "Come on, I'll go in with you."

Maggie stood starring at the closed door to the bedroom. Clarence had a right to his feelings, she reasoned, but once he heard her explanation of what happened he would understand, and they could move on with their lives. She just needed time alone to talk to him.

Maggie happened to be outside when he came out of the house and headed toward a 1931 red Ford truck parked under a grove of trees. He didn't bother to glance in her direction.

"Clarence!" Maggie called out. "Wait."

He stopped but didn't turn around.

Walking toward him she asked cordially, "This your truck?"

Turning towards her he said, "Yep. Got it a couple days ago."

"It's nice."

Clarence patted the hood. "Needed some work done on it, but I got it running smooth now. Pretty reliable. It will come in real handy for me on the farm.

"That's good."

"Yep, it's good when you can find something reliable."

Maggie ignored the intended jab aimed at her. "Aren't you glad to see me?" she asked bluntly. "You're treating me like a stranger."

"Ain't you?" He replied grimly.

"Ain't I mean aren't I what?"

Clarence looked away for a moment. His face was contorted with fury when he turned back around. "A stranger. You stopped writing, Maggie. You broke your promise. You cut me out of your life. I thought I knew you. Guess I was wrong all along."

"Clarence..." Maggie began then stopped, her hands pausing in midair. The conversation wasn't going as well as she had hoped. It was going to be difficult to explain to him what happened. How could she tell him that her friend hid his letters from her on purpose to set her up with another man? She was afraid Clarence wouldn't believe her. She would tell him the full story later when the time was right.

He crossed his arms across his chest and waited for her to continue.

Maggie, overcome with apprehensive, realized that maybe it was too soon to talk to him. She should have waited a day or two, but she needed to set things straight as soon as she could. She could see that he was hurt, but hadn't she been hurt too thinking he had moved on.

"Clarence," she implored, "Somehow your letters got lost... I... I... never got them. I wrote you several times but when I didn't get any letters back from you, I thought it was you who had deserted me. That you found someone else. So, I stopped writing."

At least she was being honest for the most part. The letters had been lost. She didn't feel it was necessary at the time to reveal the whole details.

"Why would you even think that?" he snapped. "We had a promise. You should have kept on writing. My letters would have gotten to you, eventually."

She swallowed hard. "I know that now. What happened is in the past, Clarence. Neither one of us can change it. The only thing we can do now is pick up where we left off. I was wrong to think the worst of you." She put her hand on his shoulder, "Why don't you come back and have supper with us this evening? We can talk afterwards and straighten everything out." Studying his face, she added persuasively, "I missed you. Please come."

"Okay, I guess," he said after a moment.

Maggie noticed the tension in his face soften although he still stood rigid with his arms crossed. She considered it a small victory none-the-less to get him to agree to come back for dinner. Once she talked to him and explained everything, they could work on picking up their shattered pieces.

"Good," Maggie said with relief. Then, giving him a coy look, she said, "Now, how about a welcome home hug?

He rubbed his head then shrugged his shoulders before obliging. He wrapped his arms around her in a stiff embrace, but it was enough to satisfy her.

"That's more like it," she said. "See you this evening."

"Clarence coming for supper," Maggie announced as soon as she walked into the kitchen. She went to the icebox to scan what was in it. "I want to fix something nice for him. You think Jed will kill a chicken?"

***

Bernita had seen them hugging from the window in her parent's bedroom. So, she thought to herself, Maggie don talked to Clarence already, trying to pull him back into her life. She didn't waste any time. Well, Clarence only accepted the invitation out of politeness and not because he wanted to start things back up with her. I hope he don't let her blind him to how she forgot about him while she was living her life in Philadelphia.

"Jed's too busy." Bernita said in a huff. "I guess you'll have to do the honors yourself."

Maggie gasped, "You know I never could pop the necks of those poor creatures."

"How did I ever forget?" Bernita replied sarcastically. "I guess I'll do it then." She only relented because she wanted a nice meal for Clarence as well.

33

Later that day, Bernita quickly changed out of her Sunday clothes and headed outside to stalk a young hen. She followed a plump one until she was close enough to grab it. With a quick dash, she tucked the surprised, squawking, bird under her arms. In one swift motion, she snapped the neck of the hen killing it instantly. It still squirmed and flailed around for several minutes, however, with its neck flopping to one side until she gave the head a clean chop with an axe.

Killing chickens wasn't a pleasant job for her either, but since Clarence was joining them for dinner, she put aside her aversion. She was excited even if the invitation did come from Maggie.

Because of their mother falling sick, Bernita knew it was inevitable that Maggie would come home, but still it was poor timing as far as she was concerned.

Just when Clarence was finally showing his true feelings for her. She had relinquished all hope of having a chance with him but the kiss on the porch changed everything. It was proof that he had feelings for her. Then Maggie shows up and once again she's put on the back burner. She could only hope that he wouldn't let Maggie wrap him around her fingers again. She did him wrong. Discarding him as if he was dirty dishwater and then having the nerve to just waltz back home as if nothing ever happened. Who she thinks she is? Bernita fumed to herself. She can't play with people's feelings like that.

Bernita solicited Jed's help to fill a large, black wash pot with water and build a fire underneath it. When she felt that the water was the right temperature, she held the bird by its feet and dipped it in and out of the scalding water a few times to loosen the feathers. She placed the hen on a table beside the wash pot and began yanking out the feathers.

The night on the porch floated into her mind as she proceeded with the chore. His kiss, warm and tender, was a kiss of hidden passion not a kiss of friendship. At last, Clarence had chosen her. She didn't want to lose him again to Maggie, but this time she would be patient. She would wait and see which way his heart led him.

Bernita started for the house with the headless, featherless chicken when the peach tree beyond the yard caught her attention. She made a mental note to come back out and pick a few of them.

***

Maggie put on one of the new outfits she bought at the boutique store in downtown Philadelphia. A pale, blue blouse with large cream and pink blossoms, and navy blue, wide legged trousers she tailored herself to flatter her small waist. She applied red lipstick and heavy black eyeliner that complimented her short bob then finished her makeover by dabbing rogue on her high cheekbones.

With dark blue earbobs and black, open-toed pumps, she was ready to make her appearance. Maggie knew dressing up for dinner would make her stick out like a sore thumb, but she did it for Clarence. It was a special occasion.

As expected, Bernita crinkled her nose and eyed her sharply when she came downstairs.

Maggie ignored her scrutiny. She refused to let Bernita's mean spirit darken her mood.

The gathering around the large oak table seemed subdued to Maggie without her mother's presence but it still reminded her of old times with the family. She didn't realize how home sick she had been without them.

To Maggie's disappointment Clarence made no comment on how she looked. In fact, he didn't talk much at all during the meal and even appeared uncomfortable sitting across from her at the table. He's probably still upset she thought. After they have their talk, everything will be right again.

"I got Ma to eat a few bites of her mashed potatoes and gravy," Bernita announced.

"Glad to hear her appetite is returning," Mr. Smith replied. "She got to get her strength back." Then, turning his attention to Maggie, he said bluntly, "Speaking of appetites, you skinny as a rail. You ain't been eating up there?"

Jed, still his witty self, interjected, "She boney because they don't have fatback gravy and grits up yonder."

Maggie dug her elbow into his ribs and laughed. "They do, too. They eat lots of grits as a matter of fact. At least the colored folks from down South do."

Rick offered his opinion. "She lost weight from shopping in all those department stores."

"Do they got lots of pretty dresses in Philadelphia?" Lulu asked.

"Lots and lots of pretty dresses. But I make my own clothes most of the time," Maggie said, then scrunched her face in mock anger at Rick.

Lulu's eyes became wide with wonder. "I'm going to Philadelphia when I get big."

"Rick, see what you don got started?" Mr. Smith said jovially, enjoying the light banter. "If all the young'uns take up and go north, me and your Ma ain't gonna have nobody to help out on the farm."

Buster, with his mouth full of food after taking a big bite out of his drumstick said, "Don't worry, Pa. I ain't never going north. I'm going live with you and Ma forever." His declaration brought a gale of laughter from everyone.

"What's it like up there?" Jed asked when the laughter subsided.

Maggie, pleased to share her experience, was quick with her reply. "Oh, it's way different. There're so many people and so much to see and do. Everybody always in such a big hurry though. They don't move slow like they do here in Hoop County. If you too slow up there, you might just get trampled on," she said with a laugh.

"You still a wanting to live up there instead of coming back home?" Her father asked.

Maggie became pensive. The question caught her off guard. She stole a glance across the table at Clarence whose gaze was focused intently on her, waiting for her reply. The answer was a resounding yes. She still wanted to live in Philadelphia, but she needed to settle the misunderstanding between her and Clarence before she asked him again to move north. Maggie cleared her throat and mumbled, "I haven't quite decided yet, Pa."

Bernita got up abruptly from the table and went to the stove. When she opened the oven a rush of heat followed by a mouthwatering aroma filled the room. Grabbing two heavy towels, she pulled out a steaming peach cobbler.

"Yum, yum," Rick said rubbing his belly. "I guess I have room in here for some of that!"

Mr. Smith held out his plate and Bernita scooped out a big portion for him. She then filled Clarence's plate with a heaping of the pie.

"Thanks," Clarence said. He put a large spoonful of it in his mouth. "This is good, Bernita. Did you bake it?" "Sure did," Bernita said proudly.

Throughout dinner, Maggie couldn't help noticing how Clarence and Bernita gazed occasionally at each other as if they held a special secret between them. Her female intuition sensed a shared affection, and she had to fight to keep the little twinges of jealousy from surfacing. She shook it off, thinking she was just reading too much into their friendship.

After all, she thought to herself, Bernita was her sister. Surely, she wouldn't betray her by going after her man behind her back. Or would she? But then Clarence, on the other hand, was smart enough not to fall for the snares of Bernita. No. She wouldn't let her insecurities get the best of her.

"When you learn how to cook, Bernita?" Maggie asked. She was impressed by how delicious the pie tasted.

"When you weren't here to do it," Bernita replied in a cool tone of voice.

Her flippant remark bought laughter from the group.

"Bernita been a big help 'round here," her father said gratefully.

"She still don't know how to milk the cow yet," Jed said, never missing a chance at a friendly jab.

Everyone laughed, except Maggie. Her attention was on how Clarence was looking at Bernita with admiration. She then focused her attention on Bernita, who sat to the right of her and saw how she regarded him with fondness. When Bernita turned to lock eyes with her, Maggie thought she detected a smirk on her face.

After supper, the men went out back to sit in the yard under the big walnut tree while the women cleared away the dishes. Maggie, eager to mend the rift between Clarence and her, rushed to finish washing the pots and pans. She didn't want to give Bernita any ammunition to start another fight with her if she skipped out on helping with the cleanup.

When she finally made it outside thirty minutes later, she was disappointed to find out he had already left.

34

Bernita was in her mother's bedroom early the next morning, giving her a sponge bath. "Almost finished, Ma. Turn your head so I can clean out your ears."

Mrs. Smith turned her head to one side. Bernita dabbed the tip of the washcloth in a bowl of water and gently swiped in her ear. Her mother turned her head to the other side to have the motion repeated.

"There. All finished. I'll help you get dressed." Bernita pulled open the dresser drawer and retrieved items of clothing.

Maggie opened the door. "Morning, Ma," she called out cheerfully.

Her mother nodded her head in greeting and smiled.

"Need some help?"

Bernita looked Maggie up and down as if sizing her up for the task, "Help me sit her up."

Together, they helped their mother to a sitting position and stuffed pillows behind her back for support. Maggie guided her mother's arms through her slip. When she looked up, she caught Bernita staring at her. She tilted her head to one side and raised her brows questioningly, but Bernita just averted her eyes and reached for the pink shift lying on the bed.

As Maggie continued to help her mother she thought about the changes around the farm and in the house since she'd been away. Her father, true to his word, enclosed the back porch and built a modest but nice bathroom with a toilet, sink and clawfoot bathtub. He also bought a used tractor through President Roosevelt's New Deal program for farmers, which proved to be a big help to him.

He could now plow more rows in a day than he ever did walking behind the mule. He told her, though, that he missed plowing the mule. "The tractor making a lazy man out of me," he had said jokingly. "But I'm sho glad to say the farming don taken off again. Mo crops means mo money."

And because of the extra income, between the crops and the money she's been able to send home, her mother was now able to buy new clothes and much needed items for herself and the rest of the family.

Maggie was glad her contributions helped get her family on their feet again and out of debt. One day soon, she thought to herself, she might buy one of those washing machines in Sears for her mother.

There were also physical changes in the family in such a short few months: Lulu and Buster had grown a couple of inches taller; Jed had a few twigs of facial hair growing above his upper lip; and her parents were showing more strands of gray on their heads.

Bernita...there definitely was something different about her but other than an increased air of haughtiness she couldn't quite put a finger on it. Maggie watched Bernita out of the corner of her eye. Neither of them said much to the other as they finished dressing their mother.

Of all the changes she's noticed, however, Clarence was the one who had changed the most as far as she was concerned. It disturbed her that he didn't stick around after supper to talk to her. If he wasn't ready to talk yet, at least he could have said good-by to her. She understood his anger and disappointment, but he had to give her a chance to explain everything.

The Clarence she used to know would have been more than willing to wait all night for her if he had to. Doubts about their relationship mending stirred around in her mind.

She shook her head 'no' as if to rid her mind of the illusion that it was over. She refused to believe it. If just a spark of love presided in his heart for her, then it was enough to pick up where they left off and carry on with their lives.

***

Clarence picked up an ax and with a loud grunt drove it into the thick trunk of an eight-foot tree with such force that his father paused and looked over at him. He was on his father's new land helping him clear it of bush and trees.

Thoughts of the land he planned on buying and the house he wanted to build on it for Maggie ran through his mind with each strike of the ax. He had envisioned raising children together in a house that belonged to them. It was a dream he had to let go of now. What a fool he had been to have thought Maggie would come back to him to stay.

"You okay there, son?" his father asked with concern.

"Yeah Pa." He paused to survey his progress. "This here tree is a tough one."

"Why don't you take a break? You done fell four already."

"I'm all right. It's about to fall." As he drove the last notch into the tree his thoughts returned to Maggie. He had tried putting her behind him as best he could. She no longer wanted a life with him. He was heading in the right direction until he saw her standing in her living room. He knew that eventually the time would come when their paths would cross again, but he hadn't been prepared.

His emotions did a complete turnaround when he saw her, and he had to fight the urge to sweep her up in his arms and savor her sweet lips once again. It would have been all too easy to be swept away by the woman he had once been in love with and maybe still was.

He knew she wanted to patch things up, but Clarence reminded himself that he needed to tread with caution. The Maggie that came back home wasn't the same Maggie that left Hoop County close to a year ago. He didn't know if a renewed relationship with her would survive their differences.

He reflected to December at the church play when Bernita planted a seed in his mind that Maggie was more than likely dating other men in Philadelphia. He didn't know if it was true or not but the thought of her betraying him by dating other men weighed heavily on his mind.

He only half believed her story that her friend hid the letters. The last letter he had gotten from her went on and on about how nice it was living in Philadelphia, away from the dirt roads and picking beans in the fields. She listed all the reasons he should move up there. When he wrote back telling her that he couldn't move north, he never heard from her again. She cut him off with no explanation.

Clarence was still mulling over Maggie as he took a last swing at the tree. It wasn't lost on him of how her face lit up when she talked about Philadelphia at the dinner table. When her father asked her if she still planned on going back up yonder to live, she only said she hadn't decided yet. But her heart was in the city, not Hoop County. He could tell. She even looked like a city slicker with her hair cut short and her face all dolled up.

He figured it would be the same all over again, anyway. He would fall back in love with her and then she would up and leave, expecting him to follow. That was why he left last night instead of staying to talk to her. He needed to get away to fight back the memories before his feelings for her resurfaced.

35

"Whew. I forgot how much work there was to do around this place," Maggie said as she swept the front room. She had jumped right in helping with the chores around the house wherever she could.

Bernita, standing on a chair dusting off her mother's assortment of figurines displayed on a make-shift shelf, threw Maggie a contemptuous look. "Huh, I've been reminded of it ever since you left," she said sarcastically.

Maggie stopped sweeping and looked up at Bernita, "Why don't you stop being such a bitch?"

"What you just call me?' Bernita said narrowing her eyes and placing her hands on her hips.

Maggie blew out a long breath. She didn't want to fight with Bernita, but her patience had been pushed to the limit. "I'm tired of your nasty attitude," she said as she opened the front door and swept a pile of debris outside into the yard. "You going to hold it against me the rest of my life because I left, and you had to stay?"

Crinkling her nose Bernita replied bitterly, "Naw. Why should I hold it against you? Just because you left, and I ended up having to do all the extra chores around here?" She became engrossing again with dusting.

Matching her tone, Maggie replied, "I'm sorry you had to finally lift a finger to do a little bit of work."

"Speaking of leaving... how long you plan on staying?" Bernita asked shrewdly.

Maggie eyed her suspiciously. "Why you ask?" She knew it wasn't because she hated to see her go.

Bernita shrugged her shoulders. "Oh... just wondering when I can get the bed to myself again. I don't see why Lulu can't sleep with you anyhow."

She propped her hands on the broom and rested her chin on her hand in contemplation. "Since Ma is doing much better, I might leave next week with Rick. I need to get back to work." She then added in a low tone, "I need to talk to Clarence first, though."

"About what?" Bernita asked curiously as she stepped down off the chair.

Wary about adding too much detail Maggie said, "I'm going to ask him to join me in Philadelphia..."

Bernita didn't wait for her to finish. "Clarence wouldn't want to do that!"

The explosive reaction took Maggie by surprise. She tilted her head to one side and studied Bernita closely. "How do you know?"

"Because he just can't up and leave. His Pa just brought land, and he needs Clarence to help him clear it off."

Maggie stared at her in disbelief before asking suspiciously, "Why are you so concerned with what's going on in Clarence's life?"

Bernita averted her eyes from Maggie's glare. "He confides in me."

The uneasy expression on Bernita's face confirmed what Maggie had suspected all along. She walked toward her. "Since I've been back you two have been acting strange. What's going on between you two?"

Locking eyes with Maggie, Bernita jutted her chin forward in defiance. "What's it to you? You don't care nothing about Clarence. You treated him bad."

"You don't know what you're talking about! I did not! What make you say that?"

"Once you went up north Clarence wasn't good enough for you anymore. That's what I'm talking about! Yep. He told me all about it. Said you stopped writing him when he didn't want to move up there with you. And when you weren't no longer around it was my arms he fell into..."

"I knew something was going on with you two! How could you, Bernita? My own sister, going behind my back! You low life heifer!"

"You have no right to point your finger at me! Hump. I bet you wasn't the sweet, innocent little Maggie up yonder like everybody thinks you is! Well, you don't fool me non, not one little bit! How many men did you go out with up there? Huh?"

Her eyes shifted for a fraction of a second. But it was long enough for Bernita to pick up on. It gave her the ammunition she needed.

"Aha. I thought so," Bernita said with self-satisfaction. "Now, who's the low life heifer? You having your fun living it up while poor Clarence waiting for you to come back to him?"

"What I do is none of your business," Maggie said. "Just like Clarence is none of your business!"

Bernita put her hands on her hips and leaned forward with her face inches from Maggie's. "Oh. He's my business all right. He kissed me under the willow tree!"

On instinct, Maggie slapped her across the face. Bernita drew back a balled fist and slammed it into Maggie's chest causing her to stumble backwards. In an instant, the two sisters were engaged in a brawl, swinging fists, and pulling at each other's hair.

Jed rushed into the room. "Hey! Hey! Yall! Break it up before you wake Ma." He pulled the sisters apart and stood in-between them. "What's going on with you two?"

Ask the back stabber," Maggie hissed. "I hate you, Bernita!" She ran out of the house and kept running. When she made it to the willow tree, she sank down to the ground in utter despair.

***

Maggie and Bernita avoided each other the rest of the day. When their paths did cross, they threw each other hostile looks. The feuding between the two older sisters wasn't lost on the rest of the family. The rift between them caused tension in the Smith's household.

"What's eating at those two?" Mr. Smith asked his wife after witnessing Maggie and Bernita giving each other the cold shoulder.

"Bernita sweet on Clarence," Lulu, who was sitting on the floor cutting out paper dolls, offered. "They got into a big fight over him."

"Well, well. I guess I better have a little talk with 'em."

"No, Silas. Let 'em try to work it out for themselves first. Sometimes, affairs of the heart just got to run its course."

He nodded his head in agreement then said, "I'm sho glad you feelin better, Gertie. You gonna be back to raising a racket around here in no time."

<h1 style="text-align:center">36</h1>

The following day, Maggie cornered Clarence in the field where the family was planting a row of beans.

"Clarence," she whispered in a low voice to keep the others from hearing her, especially Bernita. "I need to talk to you."

"I'm too busy right now. We can talk later." he said without looking at her and weeding with the hoe.

"No. We need to talk now," she replied abruptly.

Clarence stopped digging and gave her a curious look then laid the hoe on the ground.

Maggie glanced over her shoulder to make sure no one saw them leave. She led him to the path toward the willow tree.

It was a perfect, calm, cloudless day with a serene blue sky. But the weather was a stark contrast to the turmoil Maggie felt inside. To be under the weeping willow again with Clarence brought back bittersweet memories. A sad nostalgia for the way things used to be hung in the air.

She pulled a leaf off a branch and examined its long, narrow shape while gathering her thoughts. It seemed such a long time ago when they first kissed right in the spot where they were standing. She glanced at Clarence and said wistfully. "Our special hide-away. Remember how we used to love being together under this tree. We felt safe, just you and me, sheltered from the world."

Clarence cleared his throat and dug his hands into the pocket of his overalls. He inadvertently turned his side to her, as if facing her was too much to bear.

Maggie could sense he was uncomfortable. Awkward silence hung in the air, and a feeling of regret washed over her. It used to be so easy for them to be together and enjoy each other's company.

"It doesn't have to be this way," she said with conviction as she stepped closer to him. We can start over again. I still love you and if you still love me… I'm ready to be your wife."

Clarence stared straight ahead still refusing to face her.

"You still a wanting to live in Philadelphia?" He asked in a level voice.

"That's something we can talk about."

"So, let's talk. Do you plan on living up yonder in Philadelphia?" he asked again, with a hint of weariness in his voice.

"Why won't you come up for a visit, Clarence?" Maggie pleaded. "You might change your mind."

When he finally turned to face her, there was sorrow in his eyes. "I don't want to do that, Maggie. This is my home."

Her frustration mounted. She didn't want to give up her fight. Not yet. She placed a hand on his shoulder and asked, "What's keeping you here? There's way more freedom and opportunity for colored folks up North. Don't you realize that?"

"I can't just up and leave. My folks need me here. In Hoop County. I don't belong up there, Maggie. You had to do what you had to do to help your family. I have to do what I have to do to help mine's."

She angrily yanked another leaf from the tree. Their conversation wasn't turning out as she had expected. She wasn't getting through to him. Mistakenly, she had thought that once they were alone together, they could rekindle their love, but instead, Clarence acted cold and distant toward her. He remained firm and unyielding despite her pleas. Her high hopes of reuniting with him were grim and discouraging.

Maggie hadn't wanted to face the fact that he had turned his affection to Bernita. When Bernita told her about the kiss, she thought maybe she was lying. It was just her usual way of trying to get under her skin. Now she had reason to believe that she was telling the truth this time. She searched his face and asked the inevitable question weighing on her mind. "You sure there's no other reason that's keeping you here?"

Clarence furrowed his brows. "What other reason would there be?"

Tilting her head to one side, she gave him a discerning look. "I know Bernita have feelings for you. The question is do you have feelings for her? Is there something going on between you two?"

Clarence ran his hand over the top of his head and looked away.

Maggie braced herself for his answer.

He turned to meet her eyes. "I have to admit that I've become fond of her…"

But she didn't wait for him to finish. She had heard more than she wanted to hear. "What about us?" she yelled. "What about our promises? To not let anyone or anything come between us. Huh, Clarence? You made a promise to me!"

Clarence tried to placate her by grabbing her shoulders, but she jerked away from him. This time it was she who turned her back to him. To say he had become fond of Bernita spoke volumes to her. He might as well have shouted it loud from the mountain tops. It was a crushing, devastating blow to her heart. Even though she didn't want to believe it at first, deep down she knew it was a reality she had to face.

"Now it's your turn." Clarence crossed his arms and looked at Maggie quizzically. "Be honest with me. Did you go out with other men while you were up there?"

The tide turned on her without warning. His question surprised her knocking her off guard. "That. That… was different Clarence," she stammered. "I started seeing someone else when I thought things had ended between us."

"Why did you give up on us so easily?" he asked in a soft voice. "Why didn't you write Bernita and tell her you stopped getting my letters? She would've told me."

"I didn't want her to gloat over the fact that I wasn't hearing from you. What I didn't know though that she was scheming all this time behind my back to hurt me."

"Things didn't happen like you think, Maggie. We…we just became close friends."

Clarence's lack of consideration enraged her. It didn't seem to occur to him that becoming close to Bernita was something he shouldn't have done. He crossed a forbidden line. He let Bernita come between them. Her feelings didn't seem to matter to him at all.

"But my sister, Clarence? Of all the women in the county, why her? And why here? Under the willow…. Our special tree." The look of shock on Clarence's face told Maggie he didn't know she knew about the kiss under the tree. "Yeah. She told me," She added.

"Me and Bernita… It just happened. I swear I didn't mean to hurt you. I…"

"No. Don't try to explain. My sister has always been jealous of me, and you knew that. But I never imagined she would stoop so low," Maggie said in a grave voice. The emotional upheaval left her feeling overwhelmed and bewildered. She took a deep breath as if to steady herself and control her quavering voice, "Are you in love with her?"

"Maggie. Don't do this..." Clarence pleaded softly.

Because he didn't answer her question, she was left to believe the answer was yes. He was in love with Bernita. She lost the man she loved to her own sister. The sister who always tried to sabotage her in every way possible. The sister who always felt she had to compete with everything she did. Maggie's anger rose into an uncontrollable fury. She pummeled her fists into Clarence's chest. "How could you!".

He grabbed her arms and held them to her side until she calmed down and relented. "Don't blame Bernita for what happened between me and her. Just like you, I didn't think you wanted me anymore and she was there for me. I didn't intend for it to happen. Don't hate her. She's your own flesh and blood."

"Y'all both went behind my back," she said as she broke away from his grip.

"Maggie. It can no longer work between us, and Bernita is not the blame for that. You want what I can't give you. You don't want to come back here to live, and I don't want to move to Philadelphia. I want you to be happy."

She looked into his eyes and asked, "Do you still love me?"

Clarence took his time before answering and when he did, it wasn't what she wanted to hear. "I care for you

Maggie… but it won't work between us." he said in a low voice.

"Just leave!" she yelled. "I hate both of you!"

"No, Maggie." Clarence said with concern. "I don't want to leave you here all upset. I'm sorry…listen," he reached out for her, but she jerked away from his grasp.

"Leave!" Maggie yelled. She picked up pebbles from the ground and began throwing them at him.

Clarence ducked and looked at her helplessly before turning and heading back toward the path to the field.

She wasn't expecting their reunion to end like this, Maggie thought as she watched him walk away. He was supposed to declare his undying love for her and together they would walk back down the path hand in hand with a renewed promise to each other. Well, she came back to Hoop County thinking she had it all figured out, but her life took a turn in another direction.

When he was out of her eyesight, Maggie sank to the ground under the protective covering of the willow tree and buried her head in her arms. No longer able to hold back the dam of tears that had welled up in her chest, she let them roll freely down her cheeks as she sobbed in anguish. She vowed she would never forgive Bernita. Knowing Bernita like she did, she was sure she was laughing and gloating over the fact that she won.

A warm, slight breeze stirred through the branches, causing the limbs of the willow to caress her gently as if offering comfort. She stayed curled up under her favorite tree; the tree that sheltered her, the tree where she shared her most precious dreams, the tree she thought was special only between her and Clarence, for at least an hour or maybe two. She lost track of time and wasn't sure how long it had been, but she needed to be alone to lick the wounds of her broken heart.

Maggie entered her yard and was surprised to see her mother sitting in a chair beside her flower garden pulling up weeds. Her intentions had been to slip upstairs unnoticed. She wiped her tear-stained face with the back of her hand and forced a smile. "Hey, Ma," she called out with false cheerfulness. "I'm glad you out getting some fresh air. How you feeling?"

"I'm doing fine," her mother said. "What about you?"

Her words came out in a rush. "I'm okay. The weather is so nice today. I went for a walk. The Crepe Myrtle are so plentiful this time of year."

Her mother scrutinized her a moment then said, "You don't sound too sure you okay to me."

"No. I'm fine." Maggie said with conviction. But her words didn't match the look of distress on her face.

Her mother patted the wrought iron chair next to her. "Here. Come sit with me and keep me company."

Maggie sat in silence with her mother and watched as she continued pulling up stray weeds. The fragrant scent of the flowers relaxed her.

"I come out to see bout my precious," her mother said after a while. She reached for the tall horsetail weeds around her marigolds and yanked them up by the roots. "Flowers are just like people. They're peculiar creatures. They can be strong and sturdy and yet very fragile at the same time. It all depends on how they tended to. You got to pamper 'em, show 'e love, otherwise, if neglected they will just wither up on you and fade away."

"Your flowers are beautiful, Ma. You take good care with them."

"Yep, I do," Her mother agreed. She then caught Maggie off guard when she abruptly changed the subject. "Want to talk about what a bothering you?"

"Why you think something bothering me?" Maggie asked in astonishment, but she knew from experience her mother couldn't be fooled. She had an uncanny knack for picking up on when things were out of sorts with her children. "Clarence, huh?" her mother asked.

Letting out a big sigh, she knelt to the ground and absently began pulling up stray weeds around the peonies. "He doesn't love me anymore. I... I think he might be in love with someone else," she said, not mentioning Bernita as the other person. She didn't want to admit it to herself, let alone her mother.

"You still in love with him?" Mrs. Smith asked.

"Yes, mam... I guess I am."

"You guess? Honey, there ain't no guessing with love. Either you in love or you ain't. Ask yourself, is it Clarence you really love or is it your stubborn pride that don't want to let him go."

Maggie paused midway of plucking more weeds. She felt emotionally drained and exhausted. "I love him. I know I do. But he made promises to me that he didn't keep. He promised not to let anyone come between us and he did."

"I heard you and Bernita arguing the other day," her mother said nonchalantly.

Maggie gasped. She thought her mother had slept through hers and Bernita's spat. "You did?" she asked, surprised. "I'm sorry, Ma," she said as she rose from the ground and sat in the chair.

Mrs. Smith chuckled. "Y'all put up quite a racket." Then in a more serious tone she said, "You didn't deny to her that you been a courting someone up north. You can't have it both ways, Maggie, cause when you try to someone always winds up getting hurt."

"Ma, as far as that goes, I thought Clarence had moved on and found someone else... I tried to explain that to him. He stopped writing... and... well...it was all a big mistake." She threw her hands up in the air in desperation.

She had never experienced the pains of heartbreak before. She didn't know love could be so tormenting. It felt as if someone had snatched her heart right out of her chest, squashed and pounded it a few times, then stuffed it back in place. She tried to hold back the fresh tears stinging her eyes, but one lone tear escaped and trickled down her cheeks.

Her mother patted her on her knee. "When you really love someone, truly and dearly, you can get through the mistakes."

Maggie buried her head in her hands. "But how, Ma?" she asked through sobs.

"Tell me something. Do you love him enough to move back to Hoop County and be a farmer's wife?"

Maggie remained silent. Moving back home wasn't an option for her. She had expected Clarence to move to Philadelphia.

Her mother reached out to stroke a wayward lock of Maggie's hair back in place. "Look at me, baby."

Maggie slowly lifted her head.

"Sometimes thangs happen the way they are supposed to happen. There's just no rhyme or reason. Only God knows. Life don't always happen the way you want. Sometimes there's a plan bigger than yours that you have no control of. I know it might not seem like it now, honey. But everything gonna work out for the best. You wait and see."

37

Bernita sat on the bed combing and braiding her mother's hair while she reclined on pillows on her side with her eyes closed. She parted Mrs. Smith' short, curly hair in a narrow section and weaved a row of braids down her scalp. Bernita's mood was somber as she mentally relived the fight she had with Maggie.

She hadn't intended for things to get so out of hand, but her feathers had been ruffled and before she knew it, she blurted out about the kiss. The cat was now out of the bag. She remembered the look of hurt and pain on her face and felt a twinge of guilt. Well, she couldn't take it back now, Bernita thought to herself. She shouldn't have let Maggie get under her skin and just kept her mouth shut.

In fact, now that Maggie was home, she had made up her mind to step back and put her feelings aside for Clarence until she saw which direction his and Maggie's relationship went. He had to decide who he wanted. Her or Maggie. And she didn't want him if his heart was still tied to hers. She heeded Rosa's warning. She didn't want to end up just being a rebound.

She turned her mother's head to the other side and braided a new row of braids. Clarence didn't make it easy, though. He had her so confused. Is that what men did to women? She thought. Leave them in a confused ball of mess? Her emotions were in topsy-turvy.

That rainy day under the willow, if he had refused to return her kiss, she would have been willing to get him out of her mind for good, but he didn't. He kissed her as if she were the only one who mattered to him. He exposed his heart to her that day only to leave her befuddled when he said it shouldn't have happened. She had been so mad and disappointed in him for denying his feelings and treating the kiss as if it meant nothing when it was everything.

She had no other choice but to walk away from him. She couldn't make him love her. Her desire for him was simmering low… until that night on the porch.

"What's going on between you, Clarence, and Maggie?" Her mother asked out of the blue as if she had read her mind.

Startled, Bernita said, "What you mean, Ma?" She assumed her mother had dozed off like she usually did when she did her hair done.

"Don't pretend you don't know what I'm talking about," Mrs. Smith said in a lighthearted but serious tone of voice. "There's been a lot of upheaval around here and I bet Clarence right smack in the middle of it."

Bernita didn't respond right away. She didn't know how much she should reveal, but evidently her mother knew enough to put two and two together. "There's some issues between us we have to figure out, Ma."

"Blood is thicker than water. You and Maggie got to mend the ill will y'all have and do it now or else a deep wound will fester so large it will be nearly impossible to heal."

Maggie and she had their disagreements for as long as she could remember. Although they butted heads growing up, they never stopped being sisters. The friction between them this time though was different. Maybe the wound was already too deep.

Initially, she didn't give any thought of how her love for Clarence would affect Maggie, but she'd grown up in the months since Maggie's been away, partly because she hadn't been around to cast a shadow over her. Being more mature, she now had a better understanding of life.

The old Bernita didn't care about no one else's feelings. In the past only her feelings mattered, and she usually got what she wanted. Nothing or nobody was off-limits to her. Now, being wiser, she realized that other people's feelings counted too, especially her own sister.

"Ma is it true what they say that all's fair between love and war?" she asked as she finished the last braid.

"It might be but there's always a sacrifice of some sort. Why you ask such a question?

"Well…I fell in love with someone who's in love with someone else."

"Clarence, huh?"

Although shocked that her mother knew she didn't try to deny it. "Yes 'Ma. Clarence."

Her mother turned to face her. "Well one thing I know for sure is you can't help who you fall in love with but going after the man your sister love can cause a lot of problems for everyone involved."

"I didn't think about that. All I thought bout was having Clarence to myself and maybe one day marrying him."

"You think you ready?"

"Yes, mam. Most my friends are getting married. I guess it's time for me to think about it too."

"You're still young. You got time."

Bernita laid the comb and brush on the dresser and laid on the bed snuggling up to her mother. "But this is Hoop County and I'm seventeen. A lot of girls get married by the time they get my age. I can't live with you and pa forever. I thought Clarence was the perfect man for me. I thought we were meant for each other. Is it fair to give him up because of Maggie?"

"Now, maybe you and Clarence meant for each other and maybe not. But think about it this way. Can you be sure he will be around five years from now or even two years from now. No, you can't. But Maggie will be your sister until the day one of you leaves this world."

You just learning how to be a woman. It a big world out there. Back in my day girls got hitched sometimes as young as fifteen. Girls don't have to do that now days. They can take time to find out what they want out of life. I didn't want Maggie to go up north at first but now I'm glad she kept pestering us. She went to pursue her dreams. You a smart girl, Bernita, don't rush your life."

"This is my life. I have nothing else to offer."

"Don't you have dreams?"

Bernita let out a sigh and hugged a pillow to her chest.

"I don't know. Ain't too much dreaming a poor, colored girl from Hoop County can do."

"You only limited by your mind, chile. Never forget that."

She became silent as her mother's words sank in. "When I finished seventh grade," she said finally, "I wanted to go on to get higher schooling, but you and Pa couldn't afford to send me to the boarding school for colored girls. I guess it's too late now."

"It's never too late to better yourself. That something we can talk about later if that's what you really want to do. But right now, you and Maggie need to set things straight between y'all."

"I know, Ma. You're right." Bernita wondered though if their relationship was at the point of no return. The damage between them might not be repairable but she had to try to make amends.

38

The next day, Maggie pulled her suitcase out of the closet and sullenly began packing her belongings.

She will be on the train heading back to her life in Philadelphia tomorrow. Even though Clarence crushed her spirits, her mind had cleared enough for her to put things in perspective. Their talk in the barn last night helped her understand why their relationship was doomed. They had no other choice but to part ways.

Bernita, however, was a different story. Even though her relationship with Clarence was destined to fail, she'll never forgive her for going after him behind her back.

Her father had warned Clarence it was best for him not to come around until things settled down with his girls, but he didn't heed her father's advice. He had enlisted the help of Jed to lure her to the barn by telling her the cow wouldn't go back into her stall and he needed her expertise. When she entered the barn with him, she immediately saw that the cow was safe and sound.

"Is this a joke? Maggie asked confused, "Betsy is right where she needs to be."

As if on cue Clarence stepped out of the shadows. "Hey Maggie?"

The sound of his voice made her jump. "Clarence, what are you doing here? My father told you not to come around..."

"I had to see you."

She crossed her arms and leered at him. "Why?"

By now Jed had slipped out of the barn leaving Maggie and Clarence alone to hash out their differences.

A crease formed in the middle of his forehead showing his concern and worry. "I had to make sure you were alright. Our last meeting didn't end too well." He put his hands in his pockets then took them out as if not sure what to do with them. Rubbing a hand across his head he said, "I... well... I know you will be heading back to Philadelphia soon and...I.. don't want you to leave upset. I..." He blew out a breath without finishing his sentence.

Maggie sensed that it wasn't easy for him to face her again after the scene under the willow. Her heart softened with enough compassion to let her guard down. "What is it Clarence, that haven't been said already?" she said in a calmer voice.

"Even though I care a lot for you, you have to agree that it would never have worked between us. There were too many things standing in our way." Clarence took a tentative step toward her. "Maybe the mix up with the letters was meant to be. To show us that we weren't right for each other. We wanted different things out of life. You found a new life up north. My life is here. Always will be." Clarence paused and took a deep breath. "I don't want you to leave on bad terms is all."

"You're right," she said as she sat down on a crate. "We do want different things out of life. I can face that truth. But that wasn't the only thing standing between us. As you well know."

Clarence looked at her intently. "Don't be mad at Bernita. She's not the reason for us not working out."

Despite her efforts to stay calm, Maggie felt herself getting upset again at the mention of Bernita's name. "Kissing her was the ultimate betrayal. Don't you get it? She's my sister, for heaven's sake!"

Still standing with his hands tucked into the pockets of his overalls he said bleakly, "We kissed twice." Then in a louder voice filled with frustration said, "None of this would never have happened if you a kept writing. I thought we were over and done with, Maggie."

He wasn't getting the point, Maggie thought as she shook her head from side to side. It didn't matter how many times they kissed or even if they had kissed at all. He gave Bernita his heart. That was the betrayal. "Are you going to continue to court her?" Maggie asked in a quiet voice.

Clarence hesitated then replied cautiously. "I... I can't say..." In a more self- assured tone he said, "What I do know for sure is I'm ready to settle down, marry and raise a family. Ain't that what most young people look forward to?

Settling down and spending the rest of their lives with the one they love?" He continued without waiting for Maggie to answer. "I want to buy my own land to farm. Make an honest living."

"You swore under the willow tree the day before you left that you would come back to Hoop County to be my wife. So, you broke a promise too, Maggie. Seems like it only mattered what you wanted. What I wanted didn't count. But you always did think that you had the right answer to everything."

His raw accusation jolted her. "No, Clarence. That's not true. I'm not like that at all. Besides, my plan was to come back. I didn't expect to like it up there so much that I wanted to stay. But I did. It's not perfect up there but it beats living here. My future is in Philadelphia. Not in Hoop County. Not anymore." A moment of awkward silence passed between them in the shadowy barn. She had to face the stark realization that what they had started almost a year ago had come to an end. What was done was done.

Clarence ventured closer and stood in front of her. "I guess I caused nothing but trouble with you and Bernita. I swear it was the last thing I wanted to happen. I wish the best for you. I hope one day we can be friends again." He reached down and grabbed her hands. "I'm sorry it ended this way."

The distraught expression on his face showed his sincerity. That was one of his many attributes she admired in him. He was a sincere and honest man. She would miss him.

***

Bernita came up the stairs and paused in the doorway of the bedroom and watched Maggie as she folded her clothes and packed them in the suitcase. A feeling of sadness came over her. She wanted to put an end to the storm that's been brewing between them for far too long. After everything that's happened, though, she wasn't sure Maggie would talk to her. But she had to give it a shot. It might be her only chance before she left. She cleared her throat to get Maggie's attention, but her presence was ignored, making her even more apprehensive. Bracing herself, Bernita solemnly said, "Can we talk?"

Maggie picked up a folded blouse on the bed and threw it in the suitcase. "Talk. Nobody stopping you."

She stepped further into the room, "I'm... I'm sorry." Apologizing has never been an easy thing for her, but she was willing to swallow her pride and take the first step to salvage what she could of their relationship. The last few days of avoiding each other and not speaking had been agonizing. By now the whole family knew of their dispute, thanks to Lulu. The feud between her and Maggie filled the house with awkward tension. She hadn't spoken to Clarence since the fight.

"Why you sorry now?" Maggie hissed. "You've never been sorry about anything before."

"I was wrong for going after Clarence when I knew how you felt about him. I don't want you to be mad at me. I…"

Maggie abruptly stopped packing and interrupted Bernita in a loud voice with an emphasis on me. "You don't want me to be mad? You don't want me to be mad? You the one been mad at something or another your whole life. You had your issues with me, Bernita, but you didn't have to go behind my back!" She turned her back to Bernita and putting items in her suitcase.

Not one to easily cry, Bernita felt her eyes stinging with tears. Maggie was right. She had carried her anger around with her as if it was a badge of honor not realizing that it was just a cover up for the insecure, insignificant feelings she had about herself. She had never been able to put words to it before, but now she knew the root of her anger. She walked up to Maggie. "You're right. I didn't have to?" she said in a tight voice. "But did you ever stop to think that you stole him from me?"

Maggie's eyes widened. "How can you say that? It's not true. You always wanted whatever I had, Bernita. It's been that way with you ever since we were little."

"You might be right," Bernita said. "But you always got whatever you wanted. I had to ride your shirttail to get what I wanted."

"You're being so ridiculous."

"Am I? You the one who always stood out. Not me. Everything you touched turned to gold. You did no wrong in Ma and Pa's eyes. Everybody always compared me to you. People went on about you being smart and pretty. They never said those words about me."

Maggie paused. "That's not true," she said.

Bernita didn't want another fight, she needed to say what's been on her mind for most of her life. It was time to settle their differences. "It's true all right. You always got what you wanted, and it didn't matter to you that the man I wanted, you wanted too. That night at the dance, when you first met Clarence, you practically pushed me out of the way to get to him... you didn't care nothing about my feelings."

"You didn't even know him," Maggie said as she folded a skirt with her back still to Bernita.

"I did. Sort of. I met him way before you. It was at the church picnic the time you had to stay home sick. The moment I laid on him I knew he was the one for me. I felt it in my heart. Silly as it may seem I lived for the day when we would meet again."

Bernita's confession astonished her. She turned to face her and opened her mouth to say something but was lost on words.

"Once again," Bernita continued, "you got what you wanted even if it meant stepping over me and pushing me out the way. Heck. I couldn't compete with you. You wrapped Clarence so tight around your little finger, there was no chance for me. Well, I fell in love with him, too. He might not feel the same about me…yet. But I know there's something special between us. And if you can't forgive me... then I guess there's nothing else to say." Bernita turned and galloped down the stairs.

Left standing in total shock she had no idea Bernita felt the way she did about her. Her jealousy had always been obvious, especially during their teen years, but she mostly looked over her when she could and just considered her to be mean spirited and spoiled. It never occurred to her that her accomplishments through the years affected Bernita so much as to make her feel inadequate. Her past hostility toward her made a lot of sense now. Her sister failed to see in herself her own uniqueness.

The night of the dance rushed into her memory. Clarence… The adoring way Bernita looked at him as he walked toward them. The disappointed look on Bernita's face when Clarence looked beyond her and signaled her out instead.

Maggie thought back to the talk in the garden with her mother. Was she upset because of her wounded pride and the fact that Clarence turned to Bernita? Or, on some deeper level did she feel the need to compete with Bernita. She frowned and bit her lower lip in contemplation. Would she have pursued a relationship with Clarence if she had known Bernita had a crush on him?

She didn't know the answer to her questions. The only thing she knew for certain was the fact that she made a choice between following her heart or following her dream. She chose to follow her dream, and losing her heart was the price she had to pay.

She now had no choice but to accept it for what it was. As much as she wanted to hate her sister, even disown her, Bernita's apology was heartfelt. Even though her own heart was in broken pieces, she put aside her emotions and went to find her.

Moments later, she found Bernita outside sitting on the wrought iron swing. Bernita remained silent as she sat down beside her.

Maggie broke the ice and said, "We used to love to sit out here at night when we were little, swinging on this old swing and staring up at the stars. Remember those days?"

Bernita responded in a voice that was heavy with weariness, as she looked straight ahead. "Yep. We used to talk about our dreams. What we wanted to be when we grew up. I guess those days are long gone now. We're not little girls anymore."

"True. We're grown women now. But we can still dream." Maggie started the swing in a slow rhythmic motion. "How did we drift so far apart?" she asked with sincerity. The ebb and flow of life had not only put physical distance between them, but emotional distance as well. It was time to set things right.

Looking down Bernita shrugged her shoulders and said, "I don't know. Things just happens that way sometimes, I guess."

"Yeah. That's for sure. I ...," Maggie took a deep breath and blew out sharply. "I had a talk with Clarence the other day. There's no future for us anymore. We both grew apart."

Bernita lifted her head and gave her a puzzled look. "But he's in love with you."

"He was. Not so sure about that anymore." Remembering her talk with her mother she added, "Love can fade over time if it's not nurtured. We decided it's best to go our separate ways. There's nothing for us to hold onto anymore. I leave for Philadelphia in the morning and plan on staying up there."

"I guess things really got out of hand," Bernita said solemnly.

"Clarence belongs down here not Philadelphia. We broke it off…for good."

The hurt on Maggie's face didn't go unnoticed by Bernita. Surely the breakup hadn't been easy on her, yet she knew it was the right thing to do. Bernita saw her sister in a new light: person with a kind, unselfish heart. "You gonna be okay?" she asked.

"Yeah. I'll be fine," Maggie answered in a cheerful voice. "I will carry on with my life and put the past behind me and let bygones be bygones. I have my own dreams. I plan to open a dress boutique one day."

"That sounds exciting. If anybody can do it, you sho can." Bernita paused and looked at Maggie sitting beside her on the swing. It had been a long time since they sat together and had girl talk. "You so brave, Maggie, to leave Hoop County and everything you know to start a new life for yourself."

"I don't know if I would call it being brave. Leaving everything behind was scary, but I needed to spread my wings. What about you? What does the future hold for you?"

Bernita shrugged her shoulders. "I have some decisions of my own to make. Ma said we can talk about me finishing my schooling. I always wanted to be a nurse."

"Looking at the way you took care of her you'll make a good one." Maggie looked at Bernita with admiration. "You're the brave one. Nothing scares you and when there's something you want, you go after it.

You remember when we were little, maybe around seven and eight, we went down to the creek. I remember you walking across the plank over the creek to the other side, but I was too scared to follow you. I cried like a baby. You came back across, grabbed my hand, and led me across the water. I will never forget that."

Bernita laughed. "It barely covered our ankles."

"Well, that doesn't matter. It scared me just the same," she said with a laugh. "I remember after that day wishing I was more like you. Whatever the future has in store for you, you going to tackle it head on and come out a winner."

"Thanks. I appreciate you saying that."

They each became quiet in their own reflective thoughts as the swing gently rocked them back and forth. Maggie turned her head and locked eyes with Bernita, "I'm sorry I didn't think of your feelings. I had no idea you wanted Clarence, but you will always be my sister no matter what. I'm heading back to Philadelphia. Whatever you decide to do with your life I wish you the best."

***

The next morning, the Smiths were at the train station to see Maggie and Rick off. Mrs. Smith, much better as the doctor had predicted, was able to join the rest of the family to bid her two eldest children good-bye. "I packed extra biscuits in with yo chicken," she told Rick as she stuffed a brown paper bag into his hand."

Rick kissed her on her cheek. "Thanks, Ma,"

"I'll be home for Christmas," Maggie said as she went from person to person giving each one a goodbye hug.

"You best be home, young lady," her father said jovially. "Or I'll come up there to get you."

Maggie hesitated when she got to Bernita. They exchanged a knowing look before embracing in a hug. "I want you to come up to visit me," she offered.

"I will look forward to doing that."

Maggie heard the rumbling sound of the train coming towards them, followed by the loud choo choo of its whistle. Once again, she will be on the train going north. Only this time, when she steps off onto the platform in Philadelphia, she will be a different woman than the first time she arrived.

The train shuttled along the tracks and came to a screeching halt and opened its doors. As passengers began boarding the conductor yelled 'all aboard!' to signal to the train would be leaving shortly.

Maggie and Rick said quick goodbyes once again to everyone and climbed up the steps toward the colored section. They waved from their window as the train lurched into motion. Maggie giggled when she saw Lulu and Buster running alongside the train until they couldn't keep up any longer with its increasing speed.

"Well, back to the big city," Rick said as he settled into a comfortable position to relax.

"Yep. Here we come."

When a willow tree came into view as the train sped through the countryside, Maggie recalled what she read it symbolized from a book she checked out of the library; resilient, enduring, new life, the ability to survive in the worst of storms. She watched with bittersweet nostalgia as the tree grew smaller and smaller, then disappeared from her sight.

***

Maggie took the taxi with Rick to his apartment when they arrived back in the city. The first thing she did when she got there was to call Yvonne. She wasn't sure if the scene she had with her before she left had affected their friendship and didn't want to barge in if she was no longer welcome. As for herself, she figured she might as well forgive and forget. That was the only sensible thing to do at this point in her life. Forgive and keep moving on.

"Hello, Yvonne?" Maggie said into the phone. "Yes, I'm back in town." After a pause Maggie said, "She's doing fine. She's up on her feet again."

"Oh, Maggie I'm so glad," Yvonne said on the other line. "I been so worried."

"Yvonne?"

"Yeah?"

"Is my old room still available?"

"Why you ask, honey? Of course, it's available. Why wouldn't it be?"

"Just checking. I'll be there tomorrow evening. I want to spend time with Rick and his family while I'm over here."

"Take all the time you need. And welcome back."

***

The next evening, Maggie's taxi pulled up to the front of the apartment she shared with Yvonne. As she was waiting for the driver to retrieve her suitcase, a male voice behind her said, "Welcome back."

Maggie spun around and was pleased to see Benny standing behind her with a broad grin on his face.

"Benny! I wasn't expecting you to be here."

"I ran into Yvonne. She told me you were back in town. I wanted to be here to greet you, baby." He wrapped his arms around her in a warm embrace. "I've missed you, Maggie."

As she nestled into his arms, she admitted to herself that she had missed him, too. Sinking into his open arms was the refuge she needed.

About the Author

Jo Ellen Miller lives in Greenville SC with her terrier mix, Sam. She retired from a career as a Physical Therapist Assistant in 2019. She teaches silver sneaker exercise classes at several community centers and in her spare time enjoys oil painting.

Jo has written several short plays and enjoys reading historical romance books as well as novels pertaining to African American culture.

Willow Tree is Jo's first novel.